BATSHIFT CRAZY

NEW ORLEANS NOCTURNES
BOOK SEVEN

CARRIE PULKINEN

This is a work of fiction. Names, characters, places, and incidents are either the product of the author's imagination or are used fictitiously, and any resemblance to actual persons, living or dead, business establishments, events, or locales, is entirely coincidental.

Batshift Crazy

Contact Information: www.CarriePulkinen.com

Cover Art by GetCovers

ISBN: 978-1-957253-10-7

The shift is getting deep in New Orleans...

Gaston Bellevue has been single for one hundred years. He's a bat-shifting vampire who has amassed a fortune, runs a B and B for supes, and is living his best death in The Big Easy.

When his drunken bat collides with a windshield and he finds himself locked in a cage at an animal sanctuary, death as he knows it is about to turn batshift crazy.

Maeve O'Meara is the last bat shifter left in New Orleans...or so she thinks. When an adorable vampire bat is delivered to the Wings of Love Sanctuary in the middle of the night, she expects to find the creature there the next day. Instead, she finds tall, pale, and handsome Gaston in its place.

Maeve is terrified of vampires, but something about Gaston is so familiar. She can't help but be drawn to the mysterious man.

Until she's charged with a murder he probably committed. Or did he?

Can Gaston get his shift together and prove they're both innocent? Or have his shenanigans finally reached the end...of a stake?

"Do you still hate Mardi Gras, my friend?" Gaston Bellevue rested a hand on the parade railing to steady himself. The last woman he'd bitten had drunk her body weight in hurricanes, and the delightfully dizzy sensation he'd achieved over the course of the night was tipping into full-on drunk.

Not unusual for him, true, especially this time of year. But the night was young, and there were plenty more necks to be bitten and debauchery to be had before the sun rose. He needed to pace himself.

"I can honestly say it's my favorite holiday." Ethan grinned at his wife, Jane, his green eyes sparkling with love.

"Good answer, mister." Jane grabbed a handful of his dark gray t-shirt and planted a kiss on his lips.

Gaston chuckled. When he'd turned Ethan nearly thirty years ago, he had found himself the sire of a miserable wretch. Grumpy, self-loathing, yet the best friend he'd ever had. Ethan had met and turned Jane during Mardi Gras, and now his dearest friend was possibly the happiest vampire in the coven. A sense of pride swelled in Gaston's chest. Ethan had done well.

"What about you, Gaston?" Jane rested a hand on his shoulder, which, thankfully, slowed the tilt-a-whirl inside his head. "Captain Jack Sparrow is out in full force tonight. What's up with you and Mardi Gras?"

A high school band blasted a jazzy tune, nearly bursting his eardrums as they marched by. The flute players stopped to dance as the drum line beat out a rhythm, and the lights from the approaching float blurred into a kaleidoscope of color. Perhaps his last meal had more in her system than alcohol.

Not to worry, though. It was nothing a less inebriated snack wouldn't fix.

He ignored Jane's question—as always—and turned toward the man next to him. Gaston stood six-foot-two, while this fellow towered several inches over him, his brawny frame indicative of a human who spent far too much time attempting to acquire perfection in the gymnasium.

The man held tight to the railing, his muscular arms creating a protective cage around his intoxicated girlfriend. The sweet scents of blackberry and lime emanated from her pores, which meant she'd imbibed in cider or perhaps those flavored hard seltzers that had grown so popular amongst the humans.

While Gaston preferred to snack on women—they simply tasted better—the man was his target this time. He didn't detect much alcohol running through this behemoth's veins at all. A quick sip should be enough to sober him up, and in a crowd this dense, with Gaston's skills in glamour, no one would be the wiser.

Yes, it was against the law to bite on a main thoroughfare like St. Charles Avenue, but honestly, who would know? They were packed into the sidewalk like the bones in the Paris catacombs, the rows of spectators running at least ten deep, and nearly everyone was drunk. Besides, the vampire Council relaxed the rules of biting during Mardi Gras, allowing them the convenience of having their meals inside bars rather than in alleys or bathroom stalls. Crowded taverns were okay, but the streets were not? *Psh. The Council can shove that law right up their derrieres.*

He inched closer to his mark and swept his gaze across the crowd, looking for signs of a nosey vampire constable. Those little fuckers came to Mardi Gras in droves, hoping to find vamps behaving badly so they could write them up and exceed their monthly quotas. *Bastards.*

Luckily, the only vampires in sight were he and his friends. Gaston's head spun again. What drugs had that woman used? He couldn't wait any longer, so he activated his glamour, shielding himself from the human's prying eyes, and reached into the man's psyche, temporarily blanking his mind. At vampire speed, he sank his fangs into his prey's jugular and drank deeply.

Ack. A common O Positive laced with hints of wheatgrass and protein shakes. It was a pity the crap humans put into their bodies in an attempt to achieve perfection. He could turn them all and show them true perfection...

On second thought, then he'd be responsible for a hoard of vampires. He had his hands full enough with Ethan and Jane. When he'd had his fill of sobering O Positive, he licked the punctures, sealing the wounds, and dropped his glamour, releasing his control.

The man rubbed his neck and scratched his scalp, a look of confusion clouding his eyes for a moment before he shook his head and returned his attention to the parade.

"Satan's balls, man." Jane gaped at him. "You're either FUBAR or batshit crazy to do that right here in the crowd. Good goat cheese, are you trying to get us all staked?"

He wiped the corner of his mouth with his thumb and fought a cringe. A man *and* he was O Positive, the equivalent of eating a microwaved frozen dinner when he was accustomed to prime rib...or so he could imagine. He became a vampire long before microwaves were a thing. Or freezers.

Jane widened her eyes, expecting an answer.

"FUBAR?" he asked.

"Fucked up beyond all recognition. What's going on with you?" She crossed her arms.

He smirked. He was nowhere near that state, though he planned to be before the night was through. "When did you become such a tart feline, dear Jane?"

"It's sour puss, and ever since the Santa debacle, the Magistrate has been watching me like a creepy stalking hawk." She tossed her long brown hair over her shoulder. "I'm shooting for a seat on the Council when I reach fifty years dead, so I have to be on my best behavior."

"Seriously, man," Ethan said, "biting is never legal in crowds like this. Remember the mass panic of '03?"

He rolled his eyes. "Let us go to a bar then. You two are a moist towelette on my attempt to get flubbered." He turned on his heel and wove his way out of the crowd.

"It's pronounced foo-bar," Jane called after him.

"That is what I said," he grumbled under his breath as he broke free from the crowd.

"Step into the alley, Gaston," a gruff voice called from the shadows.

A long sigh tickled the back of his throat as he turned toward Rene Richard, enforcer of vampire law and the Magistrate's right-hand vamp. Rene's shoulder-length blond hair was slicked back into a low tail at the nape of his neck, and his brown eyes were dark and menacing. One sharp look had most vamps trembling in their tennies, but not Gaston. He had a good two hundred years on this fellow, but if he wanted his night to run smoothly, it was best to appease him.

"What can I do for you, councilman?" He bowed slightly before stepping toward him, and he sensed Ethan and Jane hovering near the alley entrance.

"Check your email." Rene crossed his arms and widened his stance as if trying to make himself appear larger...trying to intimidate a vampire two hundred years his senior. *Foolish twit.*

Gaston held in a chuckle, unable to recall the last time he felt intimidated. "I will do that as soon as I get home. Have a nice evening, Rene."

The councilman inflated his chest. "You'll check it now, or I'll haul you to the coven house by the scruff of your neck."

Jane marched toward them. "Rennie Richard, is that any way to talk to the oldest vampire in Orleans Parish?"

"If it isn't the Magistrate's little pet." He inclined his chin, looking down his nose at her. "My name is pronounced Re-NAY Ri-SHARD, and Gaston broke the law. I'll speak to him any way I deem fit."

Gaston scoffed. "I did no such thing."

"On the contrary. If you'll check your email, you will see the details of the charges. I have video evidence."

"And *how* would I check my email when I'm standing in the alley, talking to you?" Gaston had powerful glamour, but even he couldn't tap into the sky to retrieve information in his mind.

Rene closed his eyes longer than a blink, as if *he* were the one annoyed by this situation. "On your phone, you dolt."

Gaston waved off his statement. "I don't carry that annoying contraption around with me, so either tell me what law I've supposedly broken or I will be on my way. I'm far too sober to deal with the likes of you." He mumbled the last part under his breath, though it wasn't entirely true. Whatever hurricane girl had in her system, the dizzying effects were growing stronger.

"Very well." Rene clenched his jaw. "You openly bit on a public street, a crime punishable by stake."

"Hold up a hot minute." Jane stepped toward Rene, but Gaston raised a hand, stopping her.

"I appreciate you coming to my aide, *ma chère,* but this is between the councilman and me." He squared his shoulders toward Rene. "I *openly* did nothing. I used glamour to conceal my actions."

"Did you?" Rene tugged his phone from his pocket and held the screen toward Gaston. "Tell me, then. How was I able to capture it on my device?"

Gaston watched the video play and pursed his lips. His magic should have shielded him from the view of all non-magical beings...and their insuffer-able devices. "What newfangled technology is this? You have cameras that penetrate glamour now?"

Ethan stepped closer to Gaston and lowered his voice. "Dude, you didn't use glamour when you did that."

"I did so!" He whirled toward his friend, and the alley kept turning long after he stilled.

Jane clutched his arm, steadying him. "Why do you think we freaked the fuck out, man?"

His nostrils flared as he blew out a puff of air. He didn't need to breathe, of course, but some human habits were impossible to break. That drunk woman was definitely on something besides alcohol. Marijuana, perhaps? Ever since it was decriminalized, the French Quarter smelled of skunk.

"It was an accident. Nothing more than a simple mistake. At the very least, my glamour worked on the man I bit. He was more confused than a vegan werewolf when I was through with him. I will speak to the Magistrate tomorrow night and clear it up."

"You can speak to him at your trial." Rene slipped his phone into his pocket. "Lucky for you, we don't stake on the spot anymore. You'll find the details of your summons in your email. Have a nice night." He did an about-face and disappeared into the shadows.

"Satan's balls. I need a drink." Gaston smoothed his black button-up down his chest and gestured to the alley exit. "I believe we were headed to a bar."

"Maybe we should get you home and take a look at the email," Ethan said.

"Yeah, I think it's time we called it a night." Jane patted his shoulder. "You've still got that cask of AB Negative at the B and B, right? We can have a few at your place."

"That is reserved for special occasions." He narrowed his eyes. "I like you much better without the chatter of reason. I'm going to a bar. You two may do as you wish."

He stalked down the sidewalk and crossed Canal Street, the multi-lane road separating the French Quarter from the American district. The moment he stepped into the historic *Vieux Carré*, the tension in his shoulders eased. Two- and three-story buildings painted in their original shades of pastel blues, yellows, pinks, and browns lined the narrow streets, their cast-iron balconies and galleries sporting the same intricate designs as when they were first built.

Structures in the French Quarter were required

to maintain their historic exteriors, and Gaston appreciated that human law more than they could imagine. Of course, after the great fire in the late 1700s, most of the buildings burned to the ground. The current French Quarter buildings were constructed in the nineteenth century, and Gaston had fond—and not-so-fond—memories of them all. His chest pinched at the cruelest not-so-fond one, and he shoved the thought to the darkest recesses of his mind, locking it away. He'd need several drinks to keep that one subdued tonight. It was the anniversary of the worst night of his undead life.

He made his way to Bourbon Street, and his spirits lifted at the revelry. All kinds of music, from jazz to hip hop to modern rock, blasted from the bars, and the throng of people on the street was as thick as coagulated blood.

His mouth watered as a brunette in a purple V-neck sweater stumbled past him. She'd swept her hair into a messy knot on the top of her head, exposing her luscious neck, and the scent... *Mmm... Rum.*

"Wait up, old man," Ethan said in his mind.

Gaston paused, his gaze trained on his next meal, the dark, spiced scent of her blood calling to him as she hung a right on St. Peter. He followed until she slipped into a bar. *"I'll be in Pat O'Brien's."*

"Which part?"

He didn't bother with an answer. The sire/child bond would allow Ethan to find him with ease. Passing through the carriageway, Gaston's mind drifted back in time. This structure, built in the late eighteenth century, was originally a private residence, and oh, the parties the family had. Of course, Gaston hadn't quite amassed his fortune back then, and he worked for a catering company, which granted him access to the most exclusive private events. Eventually, he owned the company, along with a few restaurants, and after bumping elbows with New Orleans' elite—and sampling their privileged blood—he became one of the elite himself.

No one knew exactly where his fortune came from, and no one needed to. Times were different back then. Fewer vampiric laws meant more freedom for a creature of the night to truly be a monster if he chose.

He drifted along the slate flooring, past the main indoor bar, where he planned to stop before the night was through. To the right lay the dueling piano bar, a fun place to sit and watch drunk tourists eagerly hand over their cash and beg the musicians to play their songs. But Gaston wasn't after fun tonight. Besides, with all the wooden tables packed into the space like those little canned fish the humans ate, maneuvering from snack to snack was a pain in his ghostly white ass.

The brunette he'd set his sights on stopped at the bar for a hurricane, and Gaston's mouth watered again. The syrupy sweet, fruity rum drinks blended fabulously with the coppery taste of blood, and he couldn't wait to get a mouthful of the woman's delicious life force.

As he approached, her smile widened, the alcohol she'd consumed diminishing her self-preservation instinct. "Hello," she said.

He hadn't used an ounce of glamour, yet she allowed him to move in close enough to tuck an errant strand of hair behind her ear. "Good evening, *ma chère*. Are you here alone?"

"Ooh, are you French?"

"I was once...a long, long time ago." He activated his glamour, putting her into a temporary trance, and bit her neck. Blood flooded his tongue, and he drank deeply before licking her wounds and sealing them. He circled behind her, releasing his magic, and she rubbed her neck, turning her head from side to side as if she were confused, which she probably was. She'd just lost half a minute and half a pint of blood.

He drank from three more women before Ethan and Jane caught up to him. "I sense one who's alcohol-free at the table over there, young one." After an unfortunate accident in his living years, Ethan never partook in the drink. "And plenty for you as well, dear Jane. Join the party, won't you?"

She looked at Ethan. "I could use a drink."

"I'm a little thirsty myself." He clapped Gaston on the shoulder. "Ten more minutes, and then we're taking you home."

Gaston chuckled. As if two fledglings had any chance of forcing him to go anywhere. His friends slunk into the crowd, and Gaston found a woman drinking whiskey neat, another of his favorites.

His thirst was satiated, his belly full, yet as he stood there in the historic building, the awful memory of his gravest mistake clawed its way to the surface. Dear, sweet Bridgette. If only he hadn't been so selfish, she could be by his side today rather than turning to dust in a tomb.

No, he would not sink into that dark space. He needed to find someone who was flubbered...er... fubered... *Gah!* Whatever slang word Jane had used to mean someone who couldn't remember her own name.

He stalked into the main indoor bar and hit the jackpot. A blonde sat on a stool, her head propped on her hand, her eyes glazed and bloodshot. A drink from her should tip him over the edge and drown his sorrow.

Yesss... He barely tasted the blood over the alcohol. This was exactly what he needed.

"Give me the keys to Genevieve." Ethan tapped his shoulder. "We're taking you home."

Gaston dropped the key fob into his palm. "You may take my car back to the B and B, but I shall fly home."

Jane rolled her eyes. "You can barely stand up straight. If you try to fly, you'll be eating pavement before you get out of the Quarter."

"Nonsense. I'm fine." And sitting in the car while these two made googly eyes at each other was the last thing he needed.

He brushed past them and headed for a dark hallway. A sign above the entrance read *Employees Only*, but he ignored it.

"C'mon, Gaston. Come with us." Jane's eyes held concern. Or perhaps it was pity. Either way, she needn't bother herself.

"I believe I told you I am fine. I've had my bat-shifting ability for more than one hundred years."

"Seriously, man," Ethan said, "you shouldn't drink and fly."

Gaston waved off their concern and transformed into a bat. He swooped out of the hallway, flapping his wings for all he was worth. Perhaps he did have a few too many, but he couldn't very well turn into his human form right here in the courtyard, could he?

He flew toward the famous fountain in the center of the space, a copper contraption shaped like a champagne glass with both water and flames engulfing it. The heat coming off it warmed his belly, but the change in air pressure made him lose his balance. He flapped wildly to regain control, and perhaps a few people screamed when he fluttered by their heads, but who cared? Plenty of mundane bats made New Orleans their home.

He clipped the side of a building with his wing as he ascended to the rooftop, throwing him off balance again. *Satan's balls.* He had to get himself together. If he were human, he could pass out on a park bench and walk home in the morning. Sadly, if he tried a stunt like that, he would be nothing more than a pile of ash when the sun came up.

He perched on the edge of the roof to gain his bearings before soaring toward his home. He hated to admit Jane and Ethan were right... but they were. He couldn't make his wings flap simultaneously. Instead, he tipped from side to side before finally spiraling down.

Right into someone's windshield.

Wings spread wide, his face pressed to the glass, he could imagine he looked like a cartoon bat, tongue hanging out, cheek smushed against the surface. The impact jostled his brain, and just as he began sliding across the windshield, the driver slammed on the brakes. Gaston bounced off the hood, and then he did indeed "eat pavement" like Jane said he would.

His mouth full of gravel, he tried to tongue it out, but his vision swam, and nausea churned in his little gut. He fought to keep his eyes open as a man and a woman raced to the front of the car.

"Oh my god, James, you hit a bat!" The woman kneeled beside him.

"Don't touch it. It might have rabies." James grabbed her shoulder.

Gaston tried to take offense at his comment, but his swimming vision was beginning to tunnel. *Rabies, indeed.*

"We have to do something," the woman said.

"Should we run over it? Put it out of its misery?" James asked.

"No!" she shrieked and shot to her feet. "We have to help it. Get the shovel from the trunk. And a bag."

Why would a pair of humans be carrying a shovel and bag around in their car? He didn't have time to ponder the question. His vision was now tiny pinpricks, and his ears rang louder than an air raid siren.

"I found a bat sanctuary twenty minutes outside town," the woman said. "Let's take him there."

"Are you serious, Amy? It's late. They probably aren't even open."

"It says they have an attendant there twenty-four hours," Amy said. "We can't leave him here to die."

James huffed, and the last thing Gaston remembered was being scooped up in the shovel and dropped into a paper bag. Then, he blacked out.

TWO

Maeve O'Meara took to the sky the moment the colony of hoary bats left their roost. She was a vampire bat shifter—*not* a traditional vampire, and yes, the distinction was important. As far as she knew, she was the only bat shifter in Louisiana, thanks to the gods-awful vampire who took out her family years ago just so he could gain the ability to shift. Damn vampires and their damn parasitic habits. Living forever was never enough for them.

No, they had to take and take, sucking the life from their victims to gain their shifting abilities. Never mind the fact it had been illegal for a vampire to bite a shifter for hundreds of years. Obviously, vampires didn't care about laws.

So, yeah, Maeve was the only vampire bat in Louisiana, but the hoary colony accepted her with open wings. Of course, she cared for the furry little creatures in the Wings of Love Bat Sanctuary, nursed them back to health when they were ill, and though they were all of the non-shifting variety, they were smart enough not to bite the bat that fed them.

With the cool wind in her fur and the crescent moon shining in the sky, she followed the hoary bats above the treetops. They headed left toward a swarm of moths that would soon become their dinner, and Maeve broke from the group in search of a mammal. The heaping bowl of red beans and rice she'd eaten before she shifted didn't satisfy her bat's thirst for blood.

She spotted a feral hog sleeping near the swamp, and she swooped down, gently landing beside it before hopping onto its back and sinking her fangs into its shoulder.

Vampire bats could feed on all kinds of animals, including birds, but Maeve preferred the bigger creatures like this hog because, with her tiny fangs and small belly, they hardly noticed they'd become her meal. Vampires of the undead variety, however, had to glamour their victims into forgetting they'd been bitten. And, sure, they had their laws about not draining people and marking them so their bodies had time to replenish their blood supply before another vampire sank his fangs in, but c'mon. She'd never met a vamp who followed the rules.

Yes, she understood the irony of a vampire bat hating vampires, but when one of the arrogant, nasty suckers murdered your entire colony, you couldn't be expected to feel any other way.

With her hunger satiated, she returned to the air and caught up with the colony. They chased each other, performing feats of aerial acrobatics, and occasionally flying low enough to catch a cricket or a roach. Her enhanced auditory system in this form allowed her to hear every crunch of exoskeleton as they chewed. *Ick.* Maeve would stick to blood, thank you very much. She could only imagine picking tiny legs and antennae from between her teeth. Her fur stood on end at the thought.

Despite the crunch and munch of insects, though, flying with the colony was the highlight of her night. If her bat mouth could smile, she'd have been grinning from ear to ear.

But her elation at flying under the stars quickly turned sour. Headlights approached the sanctuary entrance, which meant one of three things: someone was lost, they found an injured bat, or the bastard who killed her family had finally found her.

Honestly, it was never the latter. She hadn't come across a vamp this far from the city the entire time she'd lived here, which was going on fifteen years now, but cautious was Maeve's middle name. Actually, it was Delilah, but you get the point.

Maeve returned to the sanctuary and slipped in through the tiny crack in her office window before shifting into human form. An obnoxious buzz reverberated through the building, and she covered her ears, still sensitive from her time as a bat. She really needed to replace that doorbell with a soft chime.

It buzzed again as she quickly threw on her clothes. "I'm coming. I'm coming." She slipped on her Converse, grabbed a wooden stake from the weapons cabinet, put a small squirt gun of holy water into her front pocket for good measure, and padded to the front of the building. Gripping the stake behind her back, she threw open the door. A couple stood on the stoop, the man holding a paper bag away from his body like he was afraid of the contents inside.

"Welcome to Wings of Love. What can I do for you?" After checking their auras for the tell-tale red glow of a vampire and finding them both mundane, Maeve put on her most welcoming smile and tucked the stake into the back of her pants. She glanced at the vehicle behind them, a brand-new Mercedes. Those cars had built-in navigation systems. No chance these two were lost.

"We hit a bat." The man shoved the bag toward her, and Maeve accepted it.

"Hit it with what?" She started to unroll the top, but the man threw his arm in front of the woman, shoving her back. As if a tiny, injured animal could actually harm them. *Sheesh.* Bats were so misunderstood.

"It flew into our windshield," the woman said. "It was still breathing when we put it in the bag."

"Interesting. A bat's echolocation system should keep it from having accidents like that. Something must be impairing it."

"Do we need to get tested for rabies?" the man asked.

Maeve fought her smile. "Did it bite you?"

He shook his head. "We didn't touch it."

"He scooped it up with a shovel," the woman said.

Oh, my. If they'd been in a work truck, she wouldn't have questioned it, but... "Why were you driving around with a shovel in your Mercedes? Going to bury a body?"

The man cut his eyes toward the woman.

Never mind. I don't want to know. "I'll take good care of this little guy. You did the right thing bringing it here. Have a nice night."

The couple darted to their car, and Maeve strode into the exam room. A tall counter with a Formica top stood in the center of the room like a kitchen island. A massive spotlight hung above it, but she didn't bother turning it on. The humans who worked there needed the light to examine injured animals. Maeve could see just fine in the dark. Contrary to popular belief, bats were not blind.

She set the bag o' bat on the counter and gently unrolled the top to peer inside. The occupant was covered in soft, brown fur, and he was about five inches long. Too big for a vampire bat, but as Maeve scooped him into her hands, her pulse thrummed. She lay him on his back—yep, he was definitely a he—and spread his wings. The adorable fuzzy face, the pitched ears, the tiny fangs protruding from his little mouth... He was overgrown, but he was, without a doubt, a vampire bat.

"Holy hellhounds," she whispered, a trill of excitement humming through her veins. "Where did you come from?"

The poor little guy was unconscious, so of course, he didn't answer. Not that he could have if he were awake…unless he was a shifter. Then again, he could've been the murdering vamp who killed her colony. He'd sucked down enough shifter blood to become one himself…all in one night. Could this be an elaborate ruse to get her alone so he could finish the job? One way to find out.

She tugged the holy water from her pocket and pointed the squirt gun at the unconscious bat. Her hand trembled, and she sucked in a shaky breath. Gripping the stake in one hand, the gun in the other, she squirted a stream of the blessed liquid onto the bat's belly. No sizzling. No anguished wails of pain. Not a vampire. Her breath came out in a rush. *Whew.*

After putting the weapons away, she rubbed her eyes and focused on his aura, trying her damnedest to see a spark of magic shimmering around him. Every now and then, a faint reddish-orange glow seemed to emanate from his fur, but it was most likely her imagination. It was nearly dawn, and she'd been up far too long. She was exhausted, and the hope that there could be another bat shifter—a vampire bat!—in New Orleans was making her see things.

"Shifter or not, I'm going to take care of you." She donned her stethoscope and listened for a heartbeat. His pulse was slow but steady. Breathing normal. She didn't detect any broken bones, though only an x-ray would confirm that. Aside from the bump on his noggin, which he probably got from head-butting the Mercedes' windshield, the bat seemed fine.

"Let's get a scan, and then you can sleep it off, okay?" She reached for the bat, and he let out a tiny groan. Her breath caught, and she ran a finger over his soft fur. "Hey there. Are you ready to wake up?"

The bat's eyes blinked open in surprise. He tilted his head, studying her before his lids fluttered shut.

Maeve laughed. "Not quite, huh?"

With a deep inhale, the bat used his wings to right himself. He narrowed his intelligent eyes at her and flapped, taking to the air in lopsided flight. He pitched to the right and then the left before smacking into the ceiling with a *thwack*. Thankfully, he caught the edge of a ceiling tile with one foot and hung on, stopping his tumble to the floor. Grabbing on with the other foot, he wrapped his wings around himself and closed his eyes.

Maeve set her stethoscope on the counter and parked her hands on her hips. "You want to sleep. Got it. We can save the x-ray for tomorrow, but I can't leave you loose in the lab all day. Come down so I can put you in a cage."

Christ on a cracker, would you listen to me? Talking to an animal as if I could reason with it. I need to get out more.

She grabbed a cloth bag from a shelf and slid a chair into position beneath the bat. "Don't be scared. I'm going to slip this over you and take you to a cage where you'll be safe." Climbing onto the chair, Maeve reached for the bat and managed to slide the sack over his body. But as she tried to pry his claws from his roost, he flapped wildly, his wing jabbing straight into her eyeball through the cloth.

"Son of a bitch!" Her vision swam, tears gushing from her eye, and she lost her balance. She tumbled backward, yanking the animal down with her and sending the bag o' bat skidding across the floor.

Her head smacked the counter, because of course it would, right? She couldn't catch the edge with her hand and break her fall. Oh, no. If she was going down, she was taking everything with her. Literally. The stethoscope, a tray of instruments, including a razor-sharp scalpel that sliced into her hand, and, of course, the offending little creature all ate tile along with her. *Oof.*

"Are you happy now? I've got a knot on my head to match yours. She scrambled to her feet. Thankfully, her shifter magic would heal her quickly, but her fond feelings for this vampire bat were quickly turning foul.

The bat sat on the sack, eyeing her with a glazed look. He was stunned for sure, and maybe a little out of it from the hubbub. All the more reason she needed to get him into a cage.

"Come on." She reached for him, and the little sucker actually had the nerve to bite her! His fangs pierced her already bloody palm, and he latched on like a miniature Dyson, sucking for everything he was worth.

"I don't think so, buddy." She grabbed him with her uninjured hand, pinning his wings to his body, and pried his fangs from her skin before tossing him into a cage and slamming the door. "Sleep it off."

The bat climbed the wall of the enclosure and hung upside down from the mesh ceiling while

Maeve washed her hands in the adjacent sink. "You're lucky shifters are immune to rabies, mister."

Her wounds already healing, she filled out the intake form, making a special note that he was a biter and should not be touched. If he was rabid, Maeve preferred to handle him. Some of the employees at Wings of Love were human and susceptible to a plethora of diseases that wouldn't affect her in the slightest.

"I'll be back when the sun sets. Behave yourself." Maeve turned out the lights to give the little guy some peace and made her way to the office.

Soft rays of morning sun rolled in through the window, and she yawned. It was time to get her nocturnal butt to bed. The day shift arrived, and she slipped out the back door, climbed the steps to her loft apartment, and crashed face-first into bed.

She had a fitful sleep, her dreams full of vampires and crazy bats, and she woke an hour before sunset. After showering and brushing her teeth, she stared at her reflection in the bathroom mirror and sighed. Her pixie cut was getting long. Wispy red locks curled at the nape of her neck when they should have been smooth against her skin. It was time for a trim, which meant a trip into the city during Mardi Gras. She was not looking forward to the traffic.

Her phone buzzed from the bedroom, and she padded across the tile and swiped the screen. "Hello?"

"Hey, girl. You up yet?" Adelaide, her rat shifter bestie, asked.

"Yeah. I need to grab some breakfast, and then I'll be down." And coffee. She couldn't function without her coffee.

"I brought chocolate chip muffins. I'll share if you can get your butt down here now."

Mmm... Her favorite. Maeve slipped on her shoes. "Something wrong?"

"That little guy you took in yesterday is going batshit crazy. I can't get him to calm down."

Fan-flapping-tastic. He was an ornery one, wasn't he? "I'm on my way." She gave her coffee maker a longing glance and headed downstairs to the sanctuary.

"It's okay, little fellow," Addy said as Maeve entered the exam room. "Maybe if you shifted, you could calm him? Vampire bat to vampire bat?"

Maeve pursed her lips and approached the cage. The bat flapped his wings faster than a sinner fanned herself in church, screeching and slamming into the door.

"You want out. Got it. But I can't turn you loose in the recovery room until I know you're healthy... and sane." She looked at Addy. "Can you grab a syringe? We need to sedate him so we can get a scan."

The bat screeched again, and his body shimmered. The reddish-orange glow she thought she imagined last night intensified and buzzed with magic. Maeve stepped back, her butt meeting the edge of the exam counter. *It can't be.*

"Holy Hades in heaven." Addy clutched her arm. "Is he a shifter?"

The buzzing bat transformed into a fully clothed man, his polished dress shoe kicking the door off the cage as he scrambled to his feet and smoothed his tailored black button-up down his stomach. He had chin-length, wavy black hair and ice-blue eyes.

Maeve froze in utter shock, her heart tumbling down into her stomach to swim through the roiling acid. His gaze locked on hers, and his eyes widened, filling with so much emotion she could have drowned in them.

"Bridgette?" His deep, sultry voice drew her in, and he blinked, his brow pinching.

Wake up, Maeve. It's a trap. She forced her gaze away from his magnetic eyes and focused on his dark red aura. She would not succumb to this fate. With a deep breath, she drew her heart back into her chest, her fight or flight instinct finally kicking in.

"Vampire! Run!" She shifted into bat form, her clothes dropping to the floor in a heap as she flew to the ceiling and clutched a tile. Apparently, Addy didn't hear her warning, because her friend just stood there, grinning at the enemy.

A bat-shifting vampire. This had to be the monster who took out her colony. She would not let him take out her friend too.

"It's you, isn't it, Bridgette?" He stepped toward her, and she hissed.

He held up his hands and chuckled. "I'm not going to hurt you. I apologize for my entrance last night. I drank from a tourist who had imbibed on more than alcohol, and I was not myself. Please forgive me." He bowed like a friggin' aristocrat from the 1700s, and her frantically beating heart slowed.

He was using his glamour. He had to be because she should have been shitting-herself-scared, but she wasn't. *Snap out of it, woman.*

"Hi." Addy gave him a little wave. "I'm Adelaide.

If you're not here to kill us, you can call me Addy. Otherwise, umm..." She cut her gaze to the door. "Maeve, maybe you should head to the office, and you know...get some supplies."

The vampire arched a dark brow, and Maeve's stomach fluttered. Was this how he did it with her entire colony? Did he draw them in with his good looks and charm, make them feel safe before he sank in his fangs and murdered them?

"I assure you I mean you no harm." He gazed up at her. "You saved my life, *ma chère*. If you hadn't taken me in, I would have burned in the sun. For that, I am in your debt."

Fangtabulous. Not only had she saved the life of a murderer, but the temptation to throw herself into his arms was so overwhelming she couldn't have stopped the shift if her life depended on it.

Which it did. *Gah!*

She dropped to the floor behind a shelving unit and returned to her human form. Unlike this gods-forsaken vampire who magically kept his clothes somewhere in his bat body, Maeve—a real shifter—was completely naked when she changed form.

She covered her boobs with her hands and rose to her full five-foot-four height. Thankfully, the shelf covered the rest of the goods because the heat in the vampire's gaze made warmth pool below her navel. If she were a man, Mr. Happy would have been standing at attention, which would have been humiliating. What the devil was wrong with her?

Think, Maeve. We need a plan. Because this vampire was about to become bloody avocado toast.

Addy backed toward her and slipped behind the shelf. "You couldn't tell he was a vampire when you took him in?" she whispered.

"Obviously not. You couldn't grab my clothes on your way to the shelf?"

"Sorry. I've never been cornered by a vampire before. Who the hell is Bridgette?"

"I have no idea other than Brigid, the Celtic goddess. He hit his head pretty hard. Maybe he's gone cuckoo for Coco Puffs, and my red hair and green eyes have him thinking I'm her."

The vampire smirked, making Maeve's pulse quicken. "Ladies, you are not cornered. Allow me to introduce myself. I am Gaston Bellevue, owner of the Bellevue Manor Bed and Breakfast and the oldest vampire in Orleans Parish." He scooped up her clothes and laid them on top of the shelf.

Maeve snatched her shirt and pulled it over her head. "You're the monster who killed my family." She continued dressing. "What's wrong? Is the shifting magic wearing off? Are you here to finish the job?" Finally, her pulse began thrumming for a reason other than her unwanted attraction to the vampire. "I escaped you before. I'll do it again, and this time, I'll finish you."

Maeve made a mad dash for the office and threw open the weapons cabinet door. Gaston appeared in the doorway in a flash, damn his vampire speed, and he cocked his head curiously at her arsenal.

"I believe we are caught in a case of mistaken identity. I swear on my mother's grave; I have never killed a bat shifter."

Maeve grabbed a stake, clutching it tightly in her hand, her logical mind telling her to ram it into his heart while she had the chance, but her own heart gave her pause, damn the blood-pumping bitch. "Yeah, right. I suppose you gained the ability to shift from what, being raised by bats?" She scoffed. "Vampires can only shift if they drink a ton of shifter blood. I'm not an idiot."

"I was essentially brought up by shifters, but they were wolves, not bats."

"Raised by wolves. Ha."

His eyes gleamed in amusement. "You don't remember me, do you?"

"I remember my family's screams. The sound of

you sucking them dry as I cowered in the cabinet beneath the sink. Why did you leave me there? So I could be your booster when the magic wore off?"

"I am not the man you believe me to be, *ma chère*. I did not gain this ability by murdering your colony or anyone else. It was a mutual partnership between myself and..." He sighed. "I mean you no harm. Please, Bridgette."

He reached for her, and she grabbed a gun full of holy water. "My name is Maeve." She squirted the water in his face, barely missing his eye.

Gaston blinked twice and flicked the liquid from his cheek with a finger. "Perhaps I should leave."

"What the ever-loving...?" She looked at the gun and then at him. How could he be unaffected? She'd bought this water from the St. Louis Cathedral. It was triple blessed.

"Why are you not sizzling like a slab of undead bacon?" She squirted him again, this time right between the eyes.

He closed his lids and pursed his lips before he spoke. "Present-day priests are not warlocks. Therefore, they do not possess the power to enchant your so-called holy water. It's nothing more than tap water that a human has prayed over."

"Son of a bitch." She tossed the gun into the trash.

"Indeed." Gaston sighed, and Addy-in-rat-form skittered past his feet to join her.

"Thanks for the help, Addy." Not that she needed it. A little voice inside her—well, it couldn't have been in her head because her brain still insisted she stake the bastard—a voice from her heart swore this vampire wouldn't hurt her. That he wasn't the one who killed her family. While she couldn't recall the killer's face—or maybe her mind had blocked out the image—she vaguely remembered a thick scar scaling the side of his cheek. This vampire had a perfectly unmarred complexion.

Gaston wasn't the murderer, but he was someone else she knew. Somewhere, somehow, she had met him before. She could feel it in her bones.

Maeve loosened her grip on the stake, but she didn't dare put it down. This calm inside her could be a trick of his magic. "If you're not the one who killed my family, why do you seem so familiar? Are you glamouring me right now?"

The sexy smirk returned to his lips, and damn it if she didn't lick her own. "I am not using any magic on you, *ma chère*. However, I must feed, so I will bid you farewell. Until we meet again, dear Maeve." He bowed, shifted into his bat, and flew out the crack in the window.

Maeve set the stake on the desk and dropped into a chair. What the ever-loving hell just happened?

CHAPTER

THREE

Gaston sat on a barstool at Nocturnal New Orleans, the first vampire bar to grace the French Quarter. Humans mingled with vampires on the dancefloor, though the mundane had no clue they were dancing neck to fangs with the actual undead. No, the humans thought it was all a ruse, that the vampires were simply mortals who never outgrew their gothic phases.

Glamour kept them from realizing what was really happening, and vampire laws ensured their safety, so no harm was done.

Gaston wasn't in the mood to drink from the vein, though. Instead, he occupied his favorite seat at the bar and sipped on a goblet of AB Negative, a rare treat. Normally, the beverage would be laced with enough whiskey to knock a two-hundred-fifty-pound gator shifter on his ass, but not tonight. He needed to keep his head clear to contemplate the woman with fiery red hair and sea-green eyes.

Maeve, the bat shifter.

Goosebumps pricked his skin at the thought of her, and his sluggish heart beat a little bit faster. Everything about her was so familiar—her voice, her face, the taste of her blood. But it couldn't be. No, it wasn't possible. There were no second chances in life or in death.

"If you scowl any harder, I'm going to give you the title of Mr. Broody McBroodypants, and Ethan won't be happy about that. He's the reigning champion three years running." Jane slid onto the seat next to him and rested an elbow on the bar. "What's on your mind, old man?"

"Nothing with which you need to concern yourself." He blew out a puff of air for emphasis.

Jane placed her hand on top of his, stilling his drumming fingers. "You can talk to me, you know?"

He gazed into her eyes, studying their chocolate brown color. Jane was a good friend. In the years since Ethan had turned her, she had become one of the best he'd ever had. But his pain was ancient, and it was his own.

"I will do my brooding at home." He tipped his head back, downing the rest of his drink, which was a shame. AB Negative should be savored, but not in the company of a prying fledgling.

"Gaston…" Jane tilted her head.

"Have a good evening, *ma chère*." He called on his magic, transforming into his bat before flying out the front door and heading home.

Genevieve, his beloved jet-black Maserati Quattroporte, sat at the back of the long drive, and he swooped over it before shifting into his vampire form in the garden. He didn't take his car out much during Mardi Gras, mainly because the traffic was horrendous and he didn't want to risk denting it again. One collision with a jolly old elf was more than enough, *merci beaucoup*. Also, Ethan refused to let him drive since he tended to imbibe on the drunkest of the drunk this time of year, but it was of no matter. His bat was all he had left of his past, and he treasured it.

He strolled through the pristinely manicured garden and admired the bubbling stone fountain he had installed when he converted his nineteenth-century Garden District mansion into the Bellevue

Manor Bed and Breakfast, a boutique establishment catering strictly to supes. A crescent moon hung in the cloudless sky, and a familiar ache expanded in his chest.

He entered the mansion through the custom rotating, light-tight door designed to keep the vampires safe when the day-dwelling supes moved about beneath the sun. Thankfully, all his guests had ventured out to enjoy the nighttime festivities, and Pierre, his trusted employee, sat in the office, watching the television. Gaston had the living room to himself.

A record player sat on an antique hutch against the far wall. Jane called the device ancient, but her concept of vampire time hadn't yet developed. He could recall the days when vinyl was the only way to enjoy music at home as if it were merely last week. He placed his favorite Bessie Smith album on the turn table and rested the needle on the record. "Nobody Knows You When You're Down and Out" played through the speaker, filling the room with music from the 1920s, both the best and worst decade of his death.

The front door spun, and he sighed. So much for time alone to ruminate on the past.

Jane and Ethan stepped into the foyer, and she

put her hands on her hips. "See what I mean? He's listening to records, and he's not drunk. Something's wrong."

"Are you okay?" Ethan followed Jane into the living room and sat on the couch.

"As I told you at the club, you need not concern yourself. I am fine and randy."

Jane giggled. "Are you now?"

Gaston poured three glasses of O Negative—he was nothing if not a good host—and handed his friends the drinks before sitting in the cigar chair across from the sofa. "Yes," he lied.

Jane sipped the blood and set her glass on the coffee table between them. "Careful. Fire can kill vampires, and your pants are ablaze."

"Seriously, man." Ethan set his glass next to hers. "Jane's right. You always get weird around Mardi Gras, but this is next level. What's going on?"

He shook his head.

Jane narrowed her eyes. "You might as well spill the tea because we aren't leaving until you do."

Gaston held her gaze and tapped his index finger against the glass. His friends had become far too perceptive.

"Does it have something to do with when you were turned?" Jane crossed her legs. "Did you become a vampire during Mardi Gras? How'd it happen?"

"I was turned in Paris long before I set foot in New Orleans." He drank from his glass, watching his friends over the rim.

"Whoa." Jane blinked twice before elbowing Ethan. "That's the most he's ever shared about his past."

Ethan raised his brows in disbelief. "Keep him going."

She nodded. "Okay. You were already a vampire when you came to New Orleans in the 1700s, so your turning has nothing to do with Mardi Gras. What happened then? Did someone try to kill you? Did you kill someone? Did you do something utterly embarrassing like pass out on the sidewalk and wake up in the hotel lobby clutching a pineapple and wearing someone else's clothes?"

Gaston rubbed his forehead. "I might as well have."

"Might as well have what? Cuddled a pineapple?"

He huffed. If he wanted any peace tonight, he would have to rip open the tea bag and toss the leaves into Jane's face. "I might as well have killed her myself. She died because of my selfishness. And now..."

Both Jane and Ethan leaned forward, resting their elbows on their knees in unison.

He waved his hand dismissively. "It is a long, painful story." One he didn't care to relive in the company of others.

"We've got all night," Ethan said.

Gaston set his glass on the table and rested his elbows on the arms of the chair, steepling his fingers. Why not? Perhaps sharing his pain could lift some of the burden. "I was in love once."

Their eyes widened.

"Hard to believe, I know." He fisted his hands before folding them in his lap. "By the mid-1800s, I had amassed a fortune, and my arrogance drove me out of the French Quarter and into this mansion. The Vampire Council was reformed, creating many of the laws we abide by today, so the means by which I gained my fortune were outlawed. But it was of no matter. I had everything a vampire could ever need. Everything except companionship."

"Pause." Jane held up a finger before gulping her drink. "You're gonna have to tell me about these fortune-amassing means sometime. My mind is spinning with ideas."

Ethan elbowed her. "We're lucky he's even telling us this. Can it, babe."

She stuck her tongue out at him before focusing on Gaston. "Sorry. Continue."

"Consider the coven as a sort of mafia. Does that suffice to quell your curiosity?"

Her mouth formed an O before she spoke. "Yep. So, you were lonely. How'd you fix that?"

The ache in his chest tightened like a vise around his heart. "I found the love of my death in the redlight district...Storyville." He looked at them both, waiting for the snide comments about him falling in love with a prostitute, but if his friends judged, they kept it to themselves.

He continued, "Her name was Bridgette, she was a bat shifter, and I adored her."

"Is she why you can turn into a bat?" Jane asked.

"Indeed, and my bat...the bat she gifted me...is the reason for her demise." A sharp pain stabbed his chest, and he leaned to the right, pressing his fist against his lips.

"Take your time," Ethan said.

He drummed his fingers on the arm of the chair. "As you know, vampires can only gain the ability to shift by drinking copious amounts of shifter blood."

Jane gasped. "Did you drain her?"

He glared. "I would never. I loved her. She allowed me to drink from her over time. Small amounts at first during our copulation, but as we fell in love, she allowed me to feed. I wanted to whisk her away. To take her far from the hard life she lived, but she was strong and independent. She insisted on paying off her debts herself, so she took a job as a waitress. I was planning to turn her, but…"

His vision blurred, and moisture gathered on his lower lids as he stared at nothing. "I could feel a bat forming inside me. The more I fed from her, the stronger it became. But I couldn't yet shift, so I waited. She agreed, saying how much she would love flying with me beneath the moonlight. Then, one night, it happened. I shifted, and it was glorious."

He swallowed the bitterness creeping up the back of his throat. "I waited until she finished work. I was to meet her outside the restaurant, and we would return to the manor where I would turn her and we would spend forever together. But I was running late, and… She never made it home."

"What happened?" Jane asked.

He closed his eyes, the memory tearing his heart in two all over again. "She was dragged into an alley and mugged. Her tips were stolen, and her throat was slit so deep...even her shifter magic couldn't heal her."

"Oh my goat cheese, Gaston." Jane's lower lip trembled. "I'm so sorry."

"I never got to fly with her." His throat thickened, and a tear spilled onto his cheek. He had never shared this story, and dredging it up now was worse than running into the sunlight at noon in August.

"The police found her killer." He forced the words over the lump in his throat. "She'd earned two dollars in tips, which is near thirty dollars today. Her life was taken for two dollars, and if I hadn't been so selfish... If I had turned her when she first asked, she would be here today. That human criminal would have simply been a meal for her, and I..."

He clamped his mouth shut.

"You couldn't have known," Jane said. "You thought you were doing the right thing."

"Tell that to Bridgette. My bat is all I have left of her." He allowed a single sob to escape his chest before wiping away his tears and straightening his spine. "Is that enough tea for you, *ma chère*?"

She nodded. "Enough to fill the harbor. I get it now. You stay drunk during Mardi Gras so you don't have to feel this pain."

"Precisely."

"So…" Ethan leaned back on the sofa. "Why are you sober now?"

Why indeed? He'd told them this much; he might as well tell them the rest. "Do you believe in second chances?"

Jane scoffed. "Let's see. A pickup truck ran me over and left me for dead. Then this hunk of undead man meat turned me into a vampire, saving my life and promising to love me forever. Nah. Second chances are for losers."

Gaston rolled his eyes. Ask a stupid question… "I believe I have found her again."

"You—" Jane tilted her head, her brows furrowing. "Continue."

"Last night, after I left you at the bar, some trouble ran into me."

"You mean you ran into trouble," Ethan said.

He ground his teeth. "No, the trouble, quite literally, ran into me. A car hit me when I was flying low, and the occupants took it upon themselves to deliver me to a bat sanctuary. The woman working there is Bridgette…no, *was* Bridgette. Her name is Maeve in this life, but the more I think about her, the more certain I am becoming that she is…*was*… my sweet Bridgette."

Ethan and Jane looked at each other, their facial expressions indicating they were communicating with telepathy. Ethan's face pinched, and Jane screwed her mouth to one side.

Gaston threw his hands into the air. "Whatever you have to say, you can say it out loud."

Jane scooted forward on the sofa and folded her hands in her lap. "Sweet cheese and rice, Alanis. You should have led with that."

"Who is Alanis?" he asked.

Jane laughed. "Alanis Morrissette? 'Ironic?'" When Gaston simply stared at her, she turned to Ethan. "He's never heard of *Jagged Little Pill*."

"I'm surprised you have," he said. "That album was before your time."

She rested her palm on his cheek. "Oh, please. Jane Devereaux is timeless. You know that."

Ethan chuckled. "That I do."

Gaston shook his head. "I do see the similarity in your situation and mine. However, there is one major difference. Maeve *is* Bridgette. I am certain of it."

Ethan pursed his lips, giving him a sympathetic look. "I was pretty damn certain Jane was someone else too, if you recall."

"Never mind it. I shouldn't have told you."

Gaston rose and paced to the window. With a few hours left before sunrise, the custom light-blocking blinds were rolled away, giving him a view of the street and the houses across from his. Aside from the cars speeding along the pavement, not much had changed since he bought this place more than a century ago.

"C'mon, babe," Jane said behind him. "We can't discount his story just because I wasn't your long-lost love. And even if Maeve isn't who he thinks she is, it might work out for them. It did for us."

"You're right." Ethan's footsteps thudded on the wood as he walked toward Gaston and clapped a hand on his shoulder. "What makes you think Maeve is Bridgette?"

"Everything about her. I remember her face, her eyes as green as the sea. Her hair is shorter, but it's the same fiery red, and her voice is like warm velvet in my ears."

"That's impressive if you can remember her face after a hundred years." Jane strolled toward the upright piano and tapped a key, filling the room with a long F.

"Are you sure you're remembering her correctly?" Ethan asked. "Or is your mind conjuring the image because of the time of year?"

Gaston grunted. Then he growled. How dare these young vampires with fewer than fifty years between them question his memory? "Follow me." He marched up the stairs to his bedroom with Ethan and Jane on his heels.

Throwing open the closet door, he flicked on the light and took a small cedar box from a high shelf. He carried it to the bed and gingerly laid it on the mattress before sinking next to it. He steeled himself for the onslaught of painful, bittersweet memories and opened the lid.

Inside lay a lock of red hair tied in a black ribbon, a ticket stub for a vaudeville show, and an old, faded photograph. His hand trembled as he reached for the picture, and he held it gently between his fingers, running his thumb over the image. Bridgette wore a black sequined flapper dress with a matching headband. A long string of pearls—real pearls that Gaston had given to her— hung from her neck, and though the photograph was black and white, he could still recall the precise shade of red on her lips.

"This is Bridgette, and yes, the woman at the bat sanctuary looks exactly like this." He returned the picture to the box and closed the lid. "Besides, a vampire never forgets the taste of his soulmate's blood."

Jane's mouth dropped open. "You bit her?"

Gaston started to answer, but she held up a hand and looked at her husband. "Wait. Is that true?"

Ethan grinned. "You smelled like fresh-baked cookies and were as sweet as maraschino cherries. I could never forget the way you tasted."

"I don't taste that way anymore?"

He shook his head. "Vampire blood doesn't taste like human blood. It's more savory. You're still a snack, though. Don't worry." He winked.

"Thank you. Okay, back to Gaston." She opened her mouth into another perfect O. "You bit her? Why are you keeping all the juicy details to yourself?"

"I believe I just told you, and it was rather embarrassing. The drugs the woman I drank from earlier in the evening hadn't worn off yet. I wasn't quite myself. She was trying to put me in a cage, and, well... I am a vampire, even in bat form."

The O returned to Jane's lips. "Your bat bit her?"

"I was unable to return to my human form until the following sunset."

She shook her head, her expression one of disbelief. "Did you talk to her?"

"Yes, but she has no memory of her previous life. She was quite shaken, and both she and the other shifter there were afraid of me."

Jane jabbed her fingers into her hair. "This is insane. What are you going to do? How are you going to win her back? When can I meet her?"

The doorbell chimed, a deep, melodic tune echoing through the empty mansion, and Gaston gestured toward the staircase. "I have yet to think that far in advance. I'm still processing this."

The bell chimed again on their way down, and Gaston stepped onto the porch to greet the visitor. Jane and Ethan followed behind, but Gaston stopped in his tracks when he recognized Alfred Mitchell, one of the Magistrate's henchmen.

Crossing his arms, he looked down his nose at the grunt. "To what do I owe the pleasure, Alf?"

Alfred tugged a pair of enchanted handcuffs from his pocket. "Gaston Bellevue, you're under arrest for the murder of Councilman Rene Richard."

CHAPTER

FOUR

"This accusation is preposterous. I demand to see the Magistrate immediately." Gaston stood behind bars in the holding cell at the vampire coven house. The chamber was nothing more than an old converted pantry, but they'd had the space enchanted to subdue magic, making escape impossible. Otherwise, he'd have turned into a bat, squeezed between the bars, and met the Magistrate in his office.

"You'll see him soon enough." Alf lounged on a chair in the kitchen and dug a dirty fingernail between his teeth. "Him and the whole Council. What's left of it."

Locked in a cell, guarded by a grunt. Gaston was far too sober to deal with this. "I will not be treated like a common criminal. I am the oldest vampire in Orleans Parish."

"Nobody gives a shit." Alf stretched his arms upward and folded his hands behind his head.

Gaston's teeth clenched with an audible click, and he struggled against the manacles confining his arms to a most uncomfortable position behind his back. It was no use. Whatever witch enchanted them, her power was unmatched. It was probably Crimson, the High Priestess herself, who'd cast the spell. He would have words with her as well.

Jeffrey, a squat vampire with bushy blond hair and a matching mustache, paced into the room. He glanced at Gaston but quickly averted his gaze, unable to look him in the eyes. Instead, he addressed Alf, "I'll escort the prisoner to the Council's chamber."

"Good." Alf unlocked the cell door. "A vampire who kills his own kind isn't worth the sludge in his veins."

Gaston saved his voice. Proclaiming his innocence to this mongrel would be a waste of breath. He followed Jeffrey out of the kitchen and into the sitting room, where Ethan and Jane sat waiting.

"Gaston!" She shot up and started toward him, but Jeffrey planted his feet, blocking her path.

"Gaston would never hurt one of his own. This is a mistake."

"I've known him my entire undead life." Ethan rose and stood next to Jane. "He's ornerier than a flea-infested werewolf and drunk half the time, but he follows the rules."

A warm fuzzy sensation spread through Gaston's chest. He didn't deserve such good friends. Truthfully, he'd turned Ethan out of boredom and loneliness. He'd thought training a fledging would be an amusing way to pass the time, but he'd grown fond of the miserable man quickly. Their relationship was much more than the typical sire-child bond. They had what Jane liked to call a "bromance," and he couldn't imagine his life any other way.

"Jeffrey, old friend. Will you kindly remove my restraints? I'm in no condition to greet the Magistrate like this."

"I'm afraid not, sir. You've been charged with murder." He opened the door and motioned for Gaston to enter the long hallway leading to the Council's chambers.

"Don't worry, Captain Jack, we've got this." Jane tried to enter the hallway, but Jeffrey blocked her path once more.

"You will wait here," he said.

"Like hell, we will." She put her hands on her hips. "I'm his lawyer; you have to let me through."

"The Vampire Council does not negotiate with lawyers."

"Then we're his alibi," Ethan said. "He was with us all night. There's no way he could have killed Rene."

Jeffrey bowed his head and gestured for them to enter. "Very well."

Gaston had traversed this hallway more times than he could count. Hell, he'd even held a seat on the Council before he'd lost his sweet Bridgette, but his will to lead had died along with his love. Never in his undead existence had he approached the Council in handcuffs. This entire ordeal was humiliating, to say the least.

The double doors leading into the chamber stood open, and the moment he passed through, Jane and Ethan flanked him. The Council sat on a raised platform at the end of the converted ballroom, the Magistrate in the center, with the rest of the Council seated in gem-encrusted chairs, two on either side of him. The seat directly to his right was empty.

Gaston and his friends stood in front of the dais,

their mouths clamped firmly shut. Silent until spoken to, as the Council rules required. The Magistrate regarded them, and sadness filled his normally menacing hazel eyes.

Elijah, the vampire to his left, rose to his feet. At two hundred years dead, Eli appeared as the epitome of popular culture's version of the horror vampire. His black robes hung loosely from his lanky form, his ashen complexion held sunken cheeks and deep-set eyes, and his shoulder-length, scraggly hair was the color of dirty dishwater.

He read from a thick piece of paper he held in both hands. "Gaston Bellevue, you are charged with the murder of Councilman Rene Richard. Unless you have proof of your innocence, you are hereby sentenced to death by stake."

I would like to see you try. Gaston eyed each of the men on the dais before scanning the faces of the spectators along the wall. In addition to Alf glaring back at him, four others had joined the hearing as witnesses.

It had been decades since he'd been in a good vampire brawl, and the urge to whoop some pasty undead ass burned in his chest.

"Nine against three," Jane's voice sounded in his mind. *"We can take them."*

Gaston glanced at Ethan and sent his thoughts to both their minds. *"I have no doubt that we could, even with my hands bound. Especially with your wicked stiletto heels, ma chère. However, I would prefer not to be responsible for overthrowing a government that normally works quite splendidly."*

"Splendidly, my left tit. This patriarchy is bullshit." Jane cleared her throat and addressed the Magistrate. "Permission to speak, Your Honor?"

The Magistrate's eyes tightened in warning, which she ignored. "This isn't the 1700s. Guilty until proven innocent is no way to govern your people."

"This is the way it has always been," Elijah answered. "This is the way it will always be."

"Not when I'm on the Council." Thankfully, Jane didn't say that out loud. Gaston was not in the mood to challenge their ways. He simply wanted to go home and brood.

"Before I present my defense," Gaston said, "I would like to know the basis for this charge. Why do you believe I am responsible for Rene's final death?"

The Magistrate took the paper from Eli and scanned the words as the other vampire returned to his seat. "We have a witness who saw you argue with Rene just off the parade route last night. Some hours later, security cameras captured a bat attacking him near the riverbank."

Gaston scoffed. "A *bat* killed a vampire? I would like to see this video."

"As you wish. Elaine?" the Magistrate called over his shoulder, and a fledgling with short brown hair and midnight eyes scurried in through a half-open door.

"Yes, Your Honor?"

"Send the evidence to Mr. Bellevue's email."

"Yes, sir."

How these old vampires had adapted to technology so quickly, Gaston would never understand. Carrying a phone in your pocket meant you were always reachable, and people expected an immediate response to the most mundane of inquiries. *Where are you? When are you getting here? Why is all the AB Negative missing from the blood bank?* The queries never ceased.

"I do not carry a mobile device."

The Magistrate shook his head like a disappointed father, and Gaston ground his teeth. He had more than one hundred years on the ruler of supernatural New Orleans. If anyone should have been in a paternal position, it was him.

"Here. You can use mine." Ethan offered his phone.

"How can I retrieve my email on your device?"

Ethan swiped the screen and opened the email server. "Just log in with your address and password."

"Mm-hmm." Gaston nodded, waiting for them to realize the ridiculousness of the request. They didn't. "And how will I do that when my hands are bound behind my back?"

The Magistrate waved at Alf, who heaved himself from a chair, grumbling as he made his way toward Gaston and unlocked the cuffs. "Don't do anything stupid."

Says the most idiotic vampire of all. Gaston growled low in his throat and accepted Ethan's contraption. He typed in his email address: *gaston-thegreat@hauntmail.com.* The password, though. What was it again? Ah, yes. He typed *Genevieve.*

Hauntmail: *The username or password is incorrect*

He tried *genevieve,* all lowercase.

Hauntmail: *The username or password is incorrect*

Oh, right. Ethan had informed him the password was too easy to guess, so he had changed it to *fangs_of_fury.*

Hauntmail: *The username or password is incorrect*

Perhaps it was *suck_my_stake.*

Hauntmail: *The username or password is incorrect. You have one more login attempt before the account is frozen.*

His grip tightened on the phone. "Which is it, then? The username or password?"

Ethan cleared his throat. "Maybe you could send the video to my account to speed things along?"

The Magistrate nodded at Elaine, and she typed on her phone. A moment later, Ethan's phone pinged, and he opened the file before pressing play and handing it back to Gaston.

A grainy video filled the screen, obviously from an outdated security camera. He knew it was outdated because he had recently commissioned a state-of-the-art surveillance system to be installed at the B and B, and the images his cameras captured appeared as crisp as real life.

In the incriminating video, Rene Richard could be seen stalking an alley. His gait was unmistakable. He had a pronounced limp from losing a leg in a fight with an alligator when he was human. He stopped halfway down the alley and turned as a fuzzy flying creature swooped in and collided with his face. The animal attacked again, and Rene flailed his arms, trying to fight off the assailant. The video glitched, turning to static for a fraction of a second. When it returned to its full resolution, a pile of ash lay where Rene once stood.

Gaston handed the phone back to Ethan. "You have a video of what appears to be a bat attacking a vampire, followed by a pile of ash. This in no way proves my guilt."

The Magistrate steepled his fingers. "You are the only person with bat-shifting abilities in Louisiana. Obviously, a small creature did not behead the councilman. The only logical conclusion is that you returned to vampire form during the camera glitch and killed him after your altercation near the parade route."

Gaston pushed his shoulders back, his lips pursing over extended fangs as he tried to keep his temper under control. *Perhaps* he could see why the Council would draw the conclusion they had, but the Magistrate knew him better than this. "The only *logical* conclusion is that I am being framed. What motive would I have for killing one of my own?"

"That is yet undetermined. Rene's phone didn't survive the altercation, so we have no record of the citations he issued last night."

Jane let out an audible sigh, and Ethan's shoulders relaxed slightly.

"Let me make certain all the chicks are standing in a queue," Gaston began.

"It's ducks in a row," Jane said into his head.

He cut a narrowed gaze toward her before continuing, "You have no motive aside from second-hand information about me having a conversation with the deceased."

"A *heated* conversation," Eli said.

"Psh. Rennie doesn't know how to have a conversation that isn't heated," Jane said. "The guy was as sour as a goblet of straight lemon juice. Whoever killed him did us all a favor."

Several councilmen nodded their agreement, but the Magistrate cocked a single eyebrow and gave Jane a look that could have turned the devil's dick into a popsicle.

"Sorry." She clamped her mouth shut. Gaston would have to master a look like that.

"If I may continue..."

The Magistrate waved a hand, telling him to wind it up.

"You have video evidence of a bat attack, which may or may not be related to the murder. A coincidence is a possibility. Or perhaps the killer has a trained bat...a witch with a familiar. It is impossible to tell." He inclined his chin, straightening his spine. "You have no definitive proof that I killed Rene."

"Yet you've supplied no proof of your innocence," Eli said. "Dawn is approaching. I move we carry out punishment immediately."

"This is ridiculous." Jane crossed her arms. "He has an alibi. We were with him half the night, and he spent the other half in a bat sanctuary outside of town. In between, he was unconscious because he was drunk and flew into someone's windshield. The humans thought he was a regular bat and took him to the sanctuary. He didn't have the time or the mental capacity to kill anyone."

The Magistrate closed his eyes for a long blink, his nostrils flaring as he let out an unnecessary breath. "If we were discussing anyone else, I would say your story is too outlandish to be true. Gaston, I will need the name of the person who took you in at the sanctuary. We will need to question him."

His stomach performed a strange feat of acrobatics inside his abdomen, twisting and turning sour at the thought. Maeve was a bat shifter with a closet full of weapons. Surely she wouldn't have... No, he refused to believe it. Her arsenal was intended for self-defense. She didn't actively hunt vampires. "There is no need to get her involved."

"I think that collision with a car must've knocked something loose in his head, Your Honor," Jane said. "Her name is Maeve, and...what was her friend's name? You said there were two shifters, right?"

His jaw clenched. "Adelaide, a rat shifter."

"Shifters. Splendid," the Magistrate said. "We don't have to deal with humans. Tomorrow at sunset, Alfred will go to the sanctuary and bring the women in for questioning. If they corroborate your story, you will be free to go."

"I don't think they'll come here willingly." Gaston gazed at the crystal chandelier hanging above the dais as he gathered his thoughts. How to put this without making Maeve look guilty? "The women were terrified of me when I was finally able to shift into vampire form."

"Alfred might not be the best person to send," Ethan said. "He can be intimidating to other supes."

"I will go," Gaston offered.

"The hell you will." Eli banged his fist on the arm of his chair. "You're spending the day in a cell."

"I know someone who could probably convince her," Jane said. "My friend Sophie has some kind of magical ability to soothe animals, shifters included. She keeps the red wolf pack and their rivals in line when they're ready to scuffle. She'll go talk to them."

"Then our coven will be indebted to the red wolf pack," Eli said. "We cannot appear as though we can't handle our business. If they refuse to come willingly, Alfred will glamour them or bring them by force."

Gaston narrowed his eyes, the thought of that oaf laying a hand on Maeve making his chest burn with rage. "Do you believe she will cooperate if she is dragged here by force? Only one of the women is necessary. Adelaide witnessed the cage I was locked in all day, and she wasn't nearly as afraid of me."

"One of the women will suffice," the Magistrate said. "Alfred will bring her here tomorrow night."

"Hold on a minute." Jane raised a hand and stepped forward. "We're trying to prove Gaston's innocence, and let me tell you, if that ogre dragged me in by the scruff of my neck, I wouldn't cooperate in the slightest. These women don't know Gaston, so why would they want to help if they're treated that way? Please let Sophie do it. Trace can go with her to make it official. He's second in command of the pack."

The councilmembers whispered amongst themselves, but the Magistrate still looked unconvinced.

Jane was right, though. If Gaston stood any chance of proving his innocence, he would need Adelaide to vouch for him. Maeve would not be involved. Not if he could help it.

"The red wolves are indebted to our coven already, Magistrate," he said. "Ethan, Jane, and I drove to Texas to retrieve a potion that saved their pack from a war with the witches. Giving them the chance to return the favor would help with coven/pack relations."

The Magistrate looked thoughtful for a moment before steepling his fingers once more. "Jane, make it happen. I expect to see your friends, along with at least one of the women, in this chamber tomorrow evening at nine. If they fail to arrive, you will be held responsible."

"Don't worry, sir. We've got this." She looked at Gaston. *"I won't let you down."*

He bowed his head in thanks, trying to keep his expression neutral. His undead life was in the hands of a fledgling vampire and her newly turned shifter best friend. What could possibly go wrong?

CHAPTER

FIVE

"How come you're not out flying with the horny bats?" Addy glided into Maeve's office and sank into a chair. Reaching behind her head, she wound her long blonde hair into a bun before tugging a band from her wrist with her teeth and securing her locks into place.

Maeve folded her arms on the desk. "They're *hoary* bats, Ad. You know that."

She shrugged one shoulder. "I'm sure some of them are horny too. One did try to get frisky with you a couple of weeks ago, didn't it?"

Her right eye twitched. She shouldn't have shared that little tidbit with her bestie. Addy would never let her live it down. "That was my fault. I should have recognized the flight pattern as a mating dance. I've been studying these bats my entire life."

Addy laughed. "Poor little guy got the shock of his life when you turned into a buck-naked woman in the middle of the cornfield, your pale ass all glowing in the moonlight like some ethereal bat goddess. If he had pants, I bet he would have shit them."

"I'm just glad there weren't any people around to see my glowing naked ass." She rested her chin in her hand. "It must be nice getting to magically keep your clothes on when you shift."

Addy grinned knowingly. "Oh, that's why you aren't out flying. You're still thinking about Mr. Tall, Pale, and Sexy. I can't say I blame you."

"It's not that he's good-looking. I mean...he *is*, but that's not why I'm thinking about him."

"Uh-huh."

She drummed her fingers on the desk. "Okay, maybe that's part of the reason, but he's a *vampire*, Addy. I hate vampires."

"Do you hate vampires, plural? Or do you hate one vampire for obvious reasons?"

Her jaw tightened. "I hate them all."

"Aside from the *one*, how many do you know?

Have you spent longer than five minutes talking to one?"

Maeve crossed her arms and leaned back in her chair. She could see where her bestie was going with this, but she couldn't be swayed. Vampires were wicked creatures. End of story. "I don't have to. They're all the same."

Addy pursed her lips. "You said you vaguely remember the guy having a scar on his face. Does that mean you hate men with scars? Or *all* men, for that matter? Do you honestly know if the bad guy was even a guy?"

"Yes, and having a scar—or a penis—doesn't mean you have to suck the life force out of people to survive."

Her brow shot toward her hairline. "Hypocrite much?"

"Well, I... But they..." Yes, she required blood to keep her bat fed, but there was a difference. "I don't kill people!" She flung her arms into the air before crossing them again.

"Neither do most vampires." Since when had Addy become the voice of reason? *More like the Devil's advocate.*

"Anyway. His attractiveness aside, I keep thinking about him because I feel like I know him.

Or, like I used to know him, but I can't remember, which is impossible. I've lived at the sanctuary ever since the massacre, so I can't possibly know him. But I feel like I do. That's crazy, right?"

Addy nodded. "Batshit."

"Of course it is."

The door buzzer sounded—it sure as hell wasn't a bell—making Maeve's skull vibrate, and she rolled her neck. "I have got to see if we have the budget for a new bell. Come on. Let's go see what the cat dragged in this time." She grabbed a stake from her weapons closet, dumped the rest of the useless so-called holy water guns into the trash, and strode out of the office.

Addy laughed and followed Maeve to the front of the building. "We get a lot of injured bats from cat attacks. Those are the creatures you should really hate."

Maeve tucked the stake into the back of her pants and peeked through the side window. Two shifters stood on the porch, their orange auras glowing with magic. She scanned the area for anyone else. They seemed to be alone, so she opened the door while clutching the stake behind her back. Hey, a girl could never be too careful these days.

"Welcome to Wings of Love. How can we help you?"

"Hi there!" The woman had long blonde hair and a bright smile. "We're looking for Maeve and Adelaide. Are they here tonight?"

Addy moved forward, practically stepping onto the porch with the shifters. "I'm Adelaide, but you can call me Addy. This is Maeve."

Maeve fought her eye roll. It would have been nice to find out what these two wanted *before* announcing their identities.

"I'm Sophie," the woman said, "and this is my husband, Trace." She gestured to the tall, muscular man beside her. "Our friend is in trouble, and we think you can help us."

Maeve narrowed her eyes. "Is your friend a bat? Because that's all we do here...we help bats."

"Actually..." Trace said, and Sophie cut him a look that made him clamp his mouth shut.

"May we come in?" Sophie asked.

"Sure!" Addy pushed the door open the rest of the way and stepped aside for them to enter. Maeve had no choice but to follow her lead.

"What kind of shifters are you?" Maeve gestured for them to follow her and returned to her office. Usually, when people brought in injured bats, they didn't stick around. The previous owner had never bothered to set up a reception area, so the office was the only place for their guests to sit.

Maeve settled into her chair while Addy perched on the corner of the desk. Sophie and Trace sank into the chairs across from them.

"We're red wolf shifters," Trace said. "I'm second in command of the New Orleans pack, and Sophie is our mediator."

"I'm a rat." Addy jabbed her thumb against her chest before pointing at Maeve. "She's a bat. How can we help?"

Sophie folded her hands in her lap. "Our friend Gaston has been accused of a crime."

At the mention of the vampire's name, a strange cooling sensation spread through Maeve's chest. Was it dread? Concern? She couldn't tell.

Sophie continued, "He was with friends the first half of the night when the crime occurred, so he has an alibi. But for the second half, he says he was here with you."

Her stomach tried to creep toward her chest, but she cleared her throat and willed it back down where it belonged. "That's true. He was in bat form when he was hit by a car. The driver brought him here, and he spent the rest of the night and the next day in a cage."

Sophie snorted. "Gaston in a cage. What a hoot! I wish I could have seen that."

"You've been summoned to the vampire's coven house to testify in his trial," Trace said. "We were sent to bring you in."

"You make it sound so ominous when you put it that way." Sophie swatted him on the arm before looking at Maeve. "We just need you to tell the Council he was here all night, and then you can leave. Easy peasy, blood bag squeazy."

"Whoa. Hold up a minute." Maeve raised her hands, palms toward them. "We aren't going anywhere near the coven house. Are you crazy? Why are you even working for them? Have they enslaved your pack?"

Trace bristled, and Sophie patted his leg, calming him. "Gaston is our friend," she said. "He mentioned your fear of vampires, so we thought it would be best for shifters to come to talk to you. We just want to help him."

She opened her mouth, closed it, and opened it again. "I'm not afraid; I'm mad as hell."

Trace cast a questioning glance toward her weapons cabinet, which she had stupidly left open.

"Your arsenal suggests otherwise. Is that gun registered?"

"We're here on supernatural business, babe," Sophie said. "Leave the human laws out of it." She looked at Maeve. "He's a cop too."

Fan-flapping-tastic. "Well, I'm sorry that your friend is in trouble, but we aren't going to the coven house."

Sophie winced. "The summons comes from the Magistrate himself. If you don't come with us, he'll send someone to take you by force."

"By force? How dare he?" Maeve shot to her feet, ready to march these traitors right out the door, but a sudden sense of calm washed over her. She blinked, trying to shake off the sensation, but it wouldn't go away. Was one of the wolves half-vampire? Their auras glowed pure orange, so they couldn't be. Shifters didn't have glamour magic, but this calmness wasn't coming from Maeve. She sank into her chair and pinched her brow. So weird.

"If you go with us, you'll be under the red wolf pack's protection," Trace said.

Sophie nodded. "We'll be with you the whole time."

"What has he been accused of?" Maeve asked.

Sophie licked her lips and glanced at her

husband before speaking. "Murder, but we know he didn't do it. Gaston is pretentious and hella goofy, but he is a great guy, and he would never hurt one of his own."

"One of his own?" Maeve scoffed. "So you need a shifter to save a man who's been accused of vampire-on-vampire crime?"

Trace looked solemn. "That's exactly what we need, what *he* needs. You two are the only ones who can help him."

Why? Why was that little voice that wormed its way up from somewhere in her chest screaming at her to help this man? It was crazy. She was a jar of mixed nuts for even considering it. One of these wolves was messing with her brain. They had to be.

"I'll go," Addy said. "You'd have to drag Maeve there, flapping and screeching, but if one of us will do, I don't mind. I'd love to see the inside of the coven house."

Sophie exhaled, her posture relaxing in relief, and the forced calm Maeve had felt a moment ago dissipated. Strangely, the asinine idea that she should help Gaston didn't dissolve with it.

"Thank you, Addy," Sophie said. "I can't begin to tell you how much I appreciate this. Gaston has helped my bestie and me out of more than a few pickles, and I am glad to be able to return the favor."

"I'll go." The words left Maeve's lips before they even registered in her brain. Addy gave her an *are you crazy?* look, and Maeve nodded. *Yes. Yes, I am.*

"I was the one who took him in. I should be the one to vouch for him." Cuckoo. She was totally bonkers.

But was she, though? Sure, she'd be in their lair, but she'd also get the chance to scope them out. Maybe the one who murdered her family was among them. Or, hell, maybe it was Gaston who did it. He was on trial for murder, so why not? *He's not the one*, the little voice told her, but she ignored it. This would be a reconnaissance mission. She could do this.

"I'm coming with you," Addy said, and Maeve's chest warmed. Her bestie was her bestie for a reason.

"Shall we?" Maeve rose and gestured to the exit.

"I wouldn't advise carrying a stake into the coven house. The vampires might take that as a threat." Trace fought a grin, and Sophie nodded as she stood.

"Right." Maeve returned the stake to the closet and closed the doors.

"Holy water guns?" Sophie gestured to the bin, which held ten plastic pistols with little black crosses drawn on them.

"Yeah."

"Why are they in the trash?"

"Apparently, modern holy water doesn't do a thing to vampires. Only a witch or warlock can make tap water into a potion to fry them like undead chicken wings."

"Huh. Who knew?" Sophie followed Trace out the door.

Gaston knew. That was who.

CHAPTER
SIX

The coven house looked nothing like Maeve expected. Instead of a black and red Victorian manor—which, if she'd thought about it, didn't exist in the French Quarter—the vampires' headquarters was a massive three-story neoclassical mansion painted a grayish-beige with white trim and green shutters. It blended in so perfectly with the surrounding buildings that she wondered if the humans ever expected they were living and working amongst murderous vampires.

Addy gripped Maeve's arm as they approached the front door. Trace rang the bell, and a deep, melodious tune echoed from inside. "That's the kind of doorbell we need at the sanctuary," Maeve whispered to her friend.

"I agree." Addy tightened her grip, and Maeve followed her gaze to see the door swing open, a short, stocky vampire blocking the entrance. Her heart high jumped into her throat. Addy's nails digging into her skin didn't help her anxiety either. She was about to venture into the den of the beast.

"We have the witness for the Bellevue trial," Trace said, his voice strong and confident.

The vampire looked from him to Sophie to Maeve and Addy before tilting his head.

Sophie elbowed her husband. "We're supposed to ask for Jeffery. Maybe this isn't Jeffery."

The vampire's lips twitched. "This way." He stepped aside and gestured for them to enter.

"I guess he is Jeffery," Maeve said, her voice an octave higher than normal.

"Must be," Sophie agreed.

They followed the vampire into a sitting room full of furniture that looked like it came straight from the 1800s. Deep burgundy upholstery covered a cherry wood chaise, and a baby grand piano sat in the corner. An ornate, oval mirror hung over the gold-encrusted wallpaper, and bronze wall sconces contained gaslit flames. *Now* the place looked like a vampire's lair.

"Wait here," Jeffery said before disappearing through a doorway.

Addy tugged Maeve down onto the chaise. "How are you feeling?"

Good question. Time for a vibe check. Her heart was slowly moving back into her chest where it belonged, but her muscles were tense in what she could only call anticipation. And since she was doing a vibe check, she might as well be honest... with herself anyway. She was excited to see Gaston, which was utterly ridiculous. She'd spent all of five minutes with him in vampire form, and when he was a bat, he'd bitten her. Excitement was the last emotion she should have been feeling, yet here she was, imagining those piercing blue eyes holding her in a heated gaze.

Gah! Get over yourself. "I'm fine."

Addy nodded. "Good. You're right. We're fine. We're under the protection of the red wolf pack, and vampires take their truces and alliances very seriously." Who was she trying to convince? Maeve or herself?

"It's true," Trace said. "There's been peace between the shifters and vamps since before I was a little swimmer in my old man's nut sack."

"If you say so." The door opened, and Maeve shot to her feet.

Jeffery held a tablet in his hands, which was weird. She'd expected a piece of parchment and a feather quill to match the decor. "I will need your full names for our records."

"Maeve O'Meara and Adelaide Duchamp." She rose onto her toes, trying to see what else he was typing on the screen, but he pressed it to his chest.

"The council will hear your testimony now."

She sucked in a full breath, straightened her spine, and followed the vampire deeper into their lair. Yep, she was certifiably batshit crazy.

At the end of the long hallway, a set of double doors opened into what might have been a ballroom when the house was built. Gas lamps enclosed in hurricane glass illuminated the space in a warm orange glow, and four men in black robes sat on a raised platform in jewel-encrusted thrones. *Wow. These dudes must think highly of themselves. Sheesh.*

Maeve's pulse thrummed, and the room stood silent. All she could hear was her own blood rushing in her ears. *Satan's balls.* If she could hear her blood, surely, with their super-mega-deluxe auditory systems, the vamps could too. And if they could hear it, they could probably smell it, and if they could smell it... Had the four of them unwittingly offered these bloodsuckers a shifter smorgasbord?

Okay, she really needed to stop calling them bloodsuckers. The derogatory term applied to all vampires, living bats like herself included, but still. What else was she supposed to call them? Fangers? She had fangs in bat form. "Murderers" was too generic. She'd have to work on a new word for the walking, talking, non-rotting corpses.

Focus, Maeve. Relax. Every muscle in her body was wound so tightly she could have cracked a walnut between her butt cheeks.

Jeffery introduced them to the Council, and Trace and Sophie moved to sit on a bench beneath a window. Now it was just the two of them, standing in the center of the room. Her hands trembled, so she clamped them into fists.

A door behind the dais opened, and Gaston strode in, flanked by two vampires in normal clothes rather than robes. He wore dark pants and a pale blue shirt that matched his eyes, and all the anxiety tying her insides—and her butt—into knots melted away when he looked at her. Crazy, she knew. He was a friggin' vampire, for fangs' sake!

Freeing herself from his mesmerizing gaze, she glanced down at his bound wrists, and an even stranger emotion stirred in her core...outrage. Why, she couldn't fathom. The man had been accused of murder, so it made sense he would be in handcuffs. But seeing him treated like a criminal made her blood boil. She wanted to run to him, to take him in her arms and tell him she was here for him.

Okay, yes, she had locked him in a cage all day, but this was different. She hadn't known he had a human...ish...side. A handsome, spellbinding, sexy-as-all-get-out side.

Hopefully vampires didn't have mind-reading abilities because her thoughts were on a runaway train headed straight for the looney bin.

One of the vampires flanking Gaston, a woman with long brown hair, smiled at her. The man on his other side narrowed his eyes, studying her, before nodding as if in agreement to something...like he was having a silent conversation in his mind with the woman.

Holy guano on a grapefruit. They *could* read minds. Her cheeks—the ones on her face—burned, no doubt turning bright red, which probably made her all the more appealing as a tasty snack. She forced her gaze toward the Royal Order of Doom and Death and willed her blood to return deep inside her body, away from her skin. Well, she tried to anyway. But as Gaston strode deeper into the room and stood a few feet away from her, she could do nothing to stop the sprinting of her pulse.

Addy slipped her hand into Maeve's and whispered, "We're fine. We've got this."

They most certainly were not fine, but her friend's touch and calming words did ease her anxiety. She no longer felt the overwhelming urge to shift and fly the hell away from this freak show.

"Maeve O'Meara." The vampire next to the head honcho rose, looking like he had just stepped off the set of *Nosferatu*. Seriously, he had extra-long, lanky fingers with pointy nails, an ashen pallor, and scraggly hair. If only he were bald. "Please tell us about your encounter with the accused."

"Umm." She cleared her throat. "Well...I didn't know he was a vampire."

"How, pray tell, did you make that mistake? Can you not see auras?" Nosferatu asked.

"No, I can. But he was in bat form and unconscious. I thought I might have seen a little orange glow, which would mean shifter, but it was late and I was tired. After a little scuffle, I locked him in a cage and went to bed."

Gaston suppressed a chuckle, the deep sound

emanating from his chest making her skin tingle. "If I may, Elijah?"

Elijah? She pictured the handsome man who played a character by that name in *The Originals*. The fictional Elijah could pass as human. This guy was the stuff of nightmares.

He nodded, and Gaston continued, "I had imbibed on a few too many inebriated tourists."

Elijah scoffed. "That's a typical Tuesday."

Gaston blew out a hard breath. "One of which had, unbeknownst to me, taken drugs in addition to the gallon of hurricanes she'd drunk. I was not myself." He turned his head toward Maeve, trapping her with his gaze once more. "And I apologize again for my behavior. I would never harm a being as lovely as you, Maeve."

The sound of her name from his lips danced across her skin like a gentle caress, and she shivered. Then she plastered on a devil-damned flirtatious smile. "I've handled my share of wild ones...way wilder than you." What in Satan's realm was wrong with her? She was most definitely *not* flirting with a vampire. They were using their glamour, making her feel more comfortable than she should. And Gaston...he must have mastered his masculine wiles and turned them into a weapon. Yeah, that was it.

"What time did you receive Gaston in your sanctuary?" Elijah's voice dragged her attention back to the matter at hand. She needed to tell them what they wanted to hear and get the hell out of this den of vipers.

"It was around three a.m. I was out flying with the hoary bat colony when the couple drove up. I saw the headlights, returned to the sanctuary, and shifted before I greeted them." She rubbed the back of her neck. "After I got him in the cage, I went home."

Addy nodded. "And he was still in the cage when my shift started the next day. He stayed until dark the following night."

Elijah's brow furrowed, his eyes calculating, and the other councilmen cut their gazes toward each other, probably reading each other's minds. Maeve's pulse kicked into another sprint. Had she done something wrong? She made eyes at Addy, who lifted her shoulders, worry tightening her features.

The man standing next to Gaston held up his phone. "The timestamp on the video is four-forty-five. There's no way Gaston could have committed the murder."

Silence engulfed the chamber. Seriously, the place was so quiet you could have heard a ghost burp, even without enhanced shifter hearing. Addy scooted closer, wrapping her arm around Maeve's bicep. "What's happening?" she whispered.

"I don't know."

The Magistrate rose to his feet, the motion so smooth and elegant it was as if he were floating on the platform. He nodded at a vampire standing next to the dais, who strode to Gaston and unlocked the handcuffs. "Gaston Bellevue," the head honcho said, "you have been found innocent. You are free to go."

"Yes!" The woman pumped her fist. "I told you we had this."

Gaston rubbed his wrists. "Much appreciated. Maeve, *ma chère*, please allow me to—"

"We are not yet finished with her," the Magistrate said as he sank onto his throne and nodded at Elijah, who stood. Before he could speak, another vampire scurried into the room and whispered something in his ear.

Why did the vamps sometimes use their words and sometimes telepathy? If Maeve could speak with her mind, she'd never open her mouth again. Well, she'd still have to eat, but other than that...

"What type of shifter are you, Ms. O'Meara?" Elijah asked.

"Umm...a vampire bat. Why?"

"And I'm a rat!" Addy's voice lifted two octaves, and her eyes shifted back and forth like they always did when she sensed danger, which made Maeve's bat hum beneath the surface, begging to take over.

She breathed deeply, willing herself not to shift, all the while thinking she'd someday look back on this moment and kick herself for not trusting her instincts. "If it pleases the court, we'll be on our way."

"Maeve O'Meara," Elijah boomed. "You have been found guilty of the murder of Councilman Rene Richard."

"What?" she screeched. "Murder? I haven't hurt a flea!" Okay, that was a lie. One of the hoaries they'd rescued recently was infested with them. She'd dipped the poor guy into a flea bath, and all the little offending suckers had floated to the surface, dead as dead could be. If that was murder, she was a serial killer.

"This is ridiculous!" Addy tightened her grip on Maeve's arm even more.

Trace shot to his feet and stormed to the center of the room to stand next to her. "These women are under the protection of the red wolf pack. Your guilty until proven innocent sham of a justice system isn't going to fly in this case."

Elijah's nostrils flared as he blew out an unnecessary breath. "Very well. You are *charged* with the murder of Councilman Rene Richard." He arched a brow at Trace.

"On what grounds?" the wolf shifter asked.

"Show him the video evidence."

A man strode toward them and handed Trace his phone. Maeve watched the screen in horror as a bat attacked the vampire's face. Then the footage turned to static for a split second. When it returned, the vampire lay in a pile of ash.

"That's not me. That's..." Her stomach dropped so hard it bounced off the inside of her asshole and lodged in her chest. "You can't prove that was me!"

Trace growled and handed the phone to Ethan. "She's right. All you have is a bat and a dead vampire. That's not proof of anything."

Gaston squared his shoulders. "I don't believe for a moment that—" The Magistrate lifted a hand, cutting him off, and he pursed his lips, obviously irritated.

If her insides weren't playing pinball against each other, she could have taken a moment to appreciate the wolf pack having her back and Gaston coming to her defense. As it was, however, she was doing good to keep her dinner from splattering all over the hardwood floor. The bat in the video was definitely not her, and if it wasn't Gaston, there was only one other person it could be.

Elijah smiled, showing fang. "No? Perhaps Maeve would like to explain the arsenal of vampire-hunting weapons our scout found in her office."

The man whispered to him again, and Elijah chuckled. "And in her bedroom. I'd say the evidence is downright damning."

Her mouth dropped open. They searched her sanctuary while she was here willingly, helping one of *them*? The nerve! "That's for my protection! One of you killed my entire colony; what do you expect me to do? Offer myself up as a snack to a murderer? It's probably the same guy!"

The Magistrate steepled his fingers like a condescending, patronizing prick. "That is a hefty accusation, young lady."

"It's true!" Her entire body trembled, and Sophie rushed toward her to rest a hand on her shoulder. Maeve instantly calmed, but she could tell the sensation didn't come from herself. She was being *made* calm, and she wasn't so sure it was for the best. Oh, and that moment when she looked back on the situation and wished she would have shifted when her bat insisted? Yeah, that moment was right freaking now.

"And how dare you send someone to search my property. You need a warrant for that. Probable cause and all that jazz. A judge has to sign off on it, you entitled piece of undead shit."

"Maeve," Addy whispered out of the corner of her mouth. "Cool it."

She needed to shut her yapper before her foot lodged in her throat, but she couldn't help herself.

The Magistrate looked like he was trying really hard not to smile, and Elijah puffed out his chest, flustering like a pissed-off peacock. "The Council is the jury," Elijah growled. "The Magistrate is judge and ruler of supernatural Louisiana. You will show respect in this chamber."

The hell she would. Not when they weren't showing her an ounce of it in return. "I am not a vampire. You have a truce with the shifters; your laws don't apply to me."

Elijah narrowed his eyes. "You murdered one of us."

"Allegedly," Sophie said, her voice strong and way more confident than Maeve felt.

He grunted. "Any truce we might have had with

your colony has been broken. You will pay for your crimes."

"Hold on," Trace said. "The truce states the colony and coven have to work together when someone is accused of breaking the terms."

"She has no colony to hold her responsible," Elijah said.

"No, but she has a pack." Sophie stepped forward next to her husband. "She's under our protection, so we'll look into it. Right, Trace?"

He nodded. "The coven will have to work with the pack to solve this crime."

Elijah scoffed. "Your alpha agrees to this? If this little bat is so important to your pack, where is your leader?"

"You're looking at him. Teresa is out of the country on a three-week sabbatical, which means I'm acting in her place. We need time to investigate the accusation before any punishment is served."

Elijah's jaw ticked, and if he were capable of turning red, he'd have looked like a ripe tomato. He sucked in a breath, ready to speak, but the Magistrate must have said something in his mind because he huffed, sat down, and crossed his arms like a pouting toddler.

"Very well," the Magistrate said. "I, too, am scheduled for a vacation. You have one month to build your case. I require Maeve to be under constant supervision. She will be assigned both a shifter and a vampire to escort her, one or both at all times."

"I'll do it," Sophie said, and Trace nodded his agreement.

"I don't need a babysitter." This was happening too fast. Her thoughts were on a tilt-a-whirl, spinning one way before shooting up and spiraling in the opposite direction. Was she really being accused of murder? "If I were blamed for every bat attack in Louisiana, I'd have been thrown in jail a long time ago."

The Magistrate arched a brow. "We can hold you in a cell here at the coven house."

A wad of cotton formed in her throat, and she swallowed it, taking all the moisture from her mouth with it. "I'll stick with Sophie, thanks."

"I volunteer to be her vampire escort," Gaston said, and a fluttering sensation formed in her stomach, which oddly settled the carnival ride spinning out of control in her gut. "I am the reason she's in this predicament, after all."

That was true. He *was* the reason she was in this mess. She'd come here to do him a favor, and now she was being charged with murder! Screw the fluttering warm fuzzies. She was livid.

"Agreed." The Magistrate rose, and the other vampires on the dais followed his lead. "Gaston, Trace, come to an agreement on where the accused will reside until we reconvene."

"Hold on." Maeve raised her hands, and the head honcho's eyes flashed a sinister red, his pupils constricting vertically like a cat...or a snake.

Gaston stepped in front of her. "Thank you, Magistrate. We will take good care of her." He bowed formally, and the Council filed out of the room.

What a load of guano. Maeve could take care of herself.

SEVEN

Gaston strode down the sidewalk at an exceedingly slow clip so the shifters could keep up. He'd have preferred to scoop Maeve into his arms and race her back to his home at vampire speed, but Trace and Sophie were the only reasons she was allowed to leave the coven house. He owed his friends his thanks and the courtesy of moving at their pace. At least, he thought he was moving at their pace.

"Why are we walking so fast?" Maeve asked. "Hey. Slow down." She clutched Gaston's wrist, and electricity seized his body, making his heart slam hard against his chest. She sucked in a sharp breath and jerked her hand away.

"I'm attempting to get you away from the coven

house before the Council changes their collective mind." He turned the corner and slowed his pace even more. "We need to discuss Maeve's accommodations." And he needed to get his head straight. Despite the evidence being so damning that Maeve might as well have ridden in on Satan's favorite hellhound to kill Rene, he refused to believe she could be responsible.

A five-piece band blasted "When the Saints Go Marching In," and a hoard of humans in glittery handmade costumes danced down the street, some singing, some shouting, all making it impossible for Gaston to think.

A young man wearing nothing more than suspenders and a speedo with his high-top sneakers grabbed Gaston's hand, attempting to pull him into the second-line parade. Had this been a normal night, and had he consumed the standard number of inebriated tourists, he would have gladly joined in the revelry. Instead, he jerked his hand free, bared his fangs, and hissed.

"Careful, tiger," Mr. Speedo said with a wink. "I like a man who's more bite than bark."

Oh, he could show him more bite than he could handle.

Ethan put a hand on Gaston's shoulder,

reminding him to focus on the issue. Maeve would need a place to stay, and he intended to make that place his home. "I suggest we gather at the B and B to discuss our next steps."

A string of plastic beads flew from the balcony above, whacking Sophie in the side of the head. She rubbed her temple and glared at the man who'd tossed it. "That's a good idea. Our car is a few blocks that way. We'll take Maeve and Addy and meet y'all there."

"This is crazy." Maeve threw her hands in the air. "I've been charged with murder, the real killer is still on the loose, and you want to go to a bed and breakfast?"

Gaston looked into her eyes, preparing to use his glamour so they could get her off the devil-damned street, but as he held her gaze, her tension visibly loosened. She felt their connection. She had to.

"The bed and breakfast is my home. It's quiet, I have blood on tap, which the vampires in our motley crew desperately need, and we can form a plan for your defense away from the prying ears of the coven."

She shook her head, maintaining eye contact. "I'm not going to your house."

"Do you have a better suggestion?"

She looked at Addy and then at Sophie and Trace. "We can go to Wings of Love. It's called a sanctuary for a reason. I need to be near my weapons."

"*Ma chère...*" He drew her attention back to him. "Your weapons are what got you into this predicament."

"No, *you* are what got me into this predicament." She jabbed her finger into his chest, and he fought a smile. Maeve was as feisty as Bridgette. Perhaps more so.

"That is true. I cannot begin to apologize for the inconvenience, but I assure you I will make this right. We will find the killer and clear your name. You have my word."

She inhaled, and her mouth opened as if she wanted to argue more, but she closed it and then opened it again. "Thank you. We can do it from the sanctuary."

Gaston cast a skeptical glance. "And when the sun comes up, do you have comfortable abodes for those of us who are allergic to UV rays? Or would we be expected to sleep in your cages...again?"

"He's right, Maeve," Addy said. "We don't have room for everyone to sit down, much less spend any time there. Let's go to his place for now. Just so we can formulate a plan to get you out of this mess."

She narrowed her eyes. "Fine. We're going from one vampire house to another. Fan-flapping-tastic."

"Until we meet again, dear Maeve." He was tempted to take her hand and press his lips to the backs of her fingers. He could still imagine the soft curve of her mouth in reaction to the gesture a lifetime ago. But this was Maeve, not Bridgette, and he did not dare.

"You are smitten," Jane said with a grin as the shifters walked away.

"You have no idea." He watched until Maeve rounded a corner and disappeared from view.

Moving at vampire speed, Gaston, Ethan, and Jane arrived at Bellevue Manor a good fifteen minutes before their guests, which gave him time to prepare refreshments and set them up in the living room. A carafe of warm O Negative, seven stemmed glasses, a charcuterie board with assorted meats and cheeses, and a bottle of wine for the shifters.

"What's the plan?" Jane poured a glass of blood and settled onto the loveseat next to Ethan. "Find the killer, make Maeve fall madly in love with you, and live happily ever after?"

Gaston chuckled. "You make it sound so simple."

She lifted one shoulder. "It doesn't have to be complicated."

"Unless Maeve really did kill Rene." Ethan stretched his arm across the back of the sofa.

"Bite your tongue, you undead Benedict Arnold." Gaston shot Ethan a look that could have turned Satan's favorite tarpit into an ice-skating rink. "She would never do such a thing unless threatened."

Jane screwed her mouth over to the side and tapped her finger against her glass. "You don't know her. Not really."

He inclined his chin. "I know her better than I know myself."

"You *knew* her," Ethan said. "This incarnation might be totally different. She's experienced different trauma; hell, she grew up in a different century."

Gaston clenched his jaw until sharp pain shot through his temple. "She did not kill Rene, and I will not entertain any more talk of it. If you want to help me find the real killer, you may stay. Otherwise..."

"Of course we're going to help," Jane said.

The rotating door spun, and Gaston shot to his

feet. Sophie entered first, then Maeve. Trace and Addy followed, but he only had eyes for the beautiful redhead who had saved his life twice.

"Welcome to Bellevue Manor." This time he took a chance. He held out his hand, and she placed hers in his palm, a surprised look crossing her delicate features. Her skin was warm against his corpse-like flesh. Delicious. "You all must be famished. Come in. Eat. Let's formulate a plan."

Maeve's hand still in his, he led them to the living room and took his usual place in the cigar chair near the record player. Maeve sat between Sophie and Addy on the couch, and Trace took the adjacent chair.

"Wow. That's quite a spread." Maeve took a cube of rosemary asiago and popped it into her mouth. "You did all this in the time it took us to drive here?"

"He was moving at warp speed. I'm Jane, by the way. This is my husband, Ethan. It's nice to finally meet you."

"Finally?" Maeve gave her a questioning look.

Jane grinned. "Gaston hasn't stopped talking about you since you met."

If you scare her away, I will personally stake you to the ground in the middle of Jackson Square and leave you for the sun to finish," he said into Jane's mind as he popped the cork on the bottle of cabernet and poured it into the shifters' glasses.

"Don't get your panties in a twist. She'll be one of the girls by the time this is through."

"Right. Well..." Trace shoved a chunk of salami into his mouth, chewed, and swallowed before continuing. "The first thing we need to do is come up with a list of suspects. Tell me about the victim. Did he have any enemies?"

Gaston scoffed. "The proper question is did he have any friends?"

"Yep," Jane said. "Rennie had his nose so far up the Magistrate's ass; it's a wonder he could smell anything but shit."

"Classy, babe." Ethan rolled his eyes.

"I'm just keeping it real."

Gaston sipped his blood and set the glass on the table. "Rene Richard got his jollies making others' lives miserable. He was always writing citations for the smallest of infractions and gener-ally wasting the Council and the Magistrate's time. Any one of them...or any one of the many vampires he has written up...would have motive. At the very least, no one shed a tear at his demise."

"So any vampire in New Orleans," Sophie said flatly. "That narrows it down."

"What about you, Gaston?" Trace asked. "Who are your enemies?"

"Aside from Rene being a thorn in my *derriere*, I have none. Do you believe someone indeed tried to frame me?" He rubbed his thumb and forefinger on his chin. "I suppose if I think back far enough, I have been in my share of fights. There could be a disgruntled individual somewhere along the way, but nothing to warrant this type of revenge."

"I don't think this is about Gaston." Maeve toyed with a toasted almond, staring at it as she rolled it between her fingers. "I think it's about me."

"You believe the man who killed your colony is responsible?" Gaston asked.

She nodded slowly and looked into his eyes. "If you are the only bat-shifting vampire in New Orleans, who else could it be? Someone had the power to make the camera glitch. Can't vampires do that with their glamour?"

"Very strong ones, yes."

Maeve shrugged. "Shifters can't do that. Unless you think a witch could be involved, it's got to be him."

"Could you identify him in a lineup?" Trace asked.

"I didn't get a good look at him." Maeve lowered her gaze. "My mother told me to hide, so I did as I was told and cowered under the kitchen sink like a child while the rest of my family was slaughtered. I've been hiding ever since."

She swallowed hard. "He must have come to New Orleans looking for me...to finish the job."

Gaston's heart ached for Maeve. Was the poor woman destined for tragedy in every lifetime? How horrible to have her entire family slaughtered in a single night.

A sinking sensation formed in his stomach. Her story was too familiar. Was it possible that their pasts and presents could be so intertwined? He knew of one vampire with the strength to commit this crime, but, last Gaston knew, he was oceans away.

No, he refused to even think of it. If the vampire who should not be named were here, he'd have sensed him by now. Hell, the bastard surely would have found Gaston. He shoved the thought out of his mind. The similarities between her story and his were nothing more than a coincidence.

Sophie tugged on her bottom lip before dropping her hand into her lap. "But if he came back for you, why would he kill Rene?"

"Perhaps Rene simply got in the way," Gaston said. "He interrupted me in my Mardi Gras revelry. It's likely he attempted to issue a citation to the killer. It is Mardi Gras season, after all. Vampires from all over the country travel here this time of year. The culprit truly could have been anyone." Because if it was who he suspected, the entire city was doomed.

Maeve's posture deflated. "What are we going to do? Your buddies of the Grand Order of Corpse and Coffin are determined to pin this on me."

Jane laughed. "I thought they were the Volturi the first time I met them."

"I can see that, though Elijah is closer to Nosferatu with scraggly mop hair."

"Oh, that's a good one," she said aloud before saying, "*I like her already,*" in Gaston's mind.

He drummed his fingers on the arm of the chair, an idea forming in the chaos of his racing thoughts. "I believe I have a solution that will clear Maeve's name. We will simply ask Rene who killed him."

"Ask him?" Maeve cocked her head. "You're forgetting the part about him being dead."

He waved a hand dismissively. "A minor inconvenience, but nothing the most powerful necromancer in the South can't overcome."

Ethan laughed. "You want *Jasmine Lee* to reanimate a vampire...for you...a vampire."

"There's no way she's going to help a bunch of vamps," Jane said. "She can't even stand to be around us."

"Perhaps not, but Asher might." Gaston looked at Maeve. "The grim reaper is a friend of mine."

She blinked twice. "And I suppose the high priestess of the witch's coven comes over for Sunday dinner every week? Is there anyone you don't know?"

"Crimson is one of my best friends," Sophie said. "Jasmine is too, so Gaston's plan just might work."

"Why wouldn't the necromancer want to help vampires?" Addy asked. "Y'all seem perfectly pleasant to me."

"Vampires have an unnatural attraction to necromancers," Gaston said. "We are drawn to her, and it outs her creeper."

"He means 'creeps her out.'" Jane rolled her eyes.

"I'll call her in the morning," Trace said. "She does work for the police all the time."

"Speaking of morning," Jane yawned. "Daylight

is fast approaching, and unless y'all want to haul my undead weight up the stairs and into a bedroom, Ethan and I need to go home. The death sleep will be pulling me under any time now."

Gaston rose and bowed at his friends. "Your assistance has been much appreciated. Trace, please keep us informed on the progress with Jasmine."

"Will do."

"Maeve, you must be exhausted. Allow me to show you to your room." He gestured to the stairs, and she rose to her feet.

"You're safe here," Sophie said, "but if you want me to stay with you, I'm happy to."

"I'll stay." Addy stood. "We can share a room."

A tiny, hesitant smile lighted on Maeve's lips as she looked into Gaston's eyes. "That's okay. I'm sure I'll be fine."

"THANK YOU, everyone. I can't tell you how much I appreciate your help." Maeve waved goodbye and followed Gaston up the stairs. His house was massive, with hardwood floors stretching down the long hallway, a deep blue runner muffling the sounds of their footsteps. Sconces shaped like oil lamps hung along the walls, their dim electric bulbs casting soft shadows across the carpet.

She'd already decided she was certifiably insane for even thinking about trusting a vampire. Telling Addy and her new wolf shifter friends they could leave her alone here took her from crazy to possibly having a death wish.

But did it really?

It wasn't that she trusted Gaston; she hardly knew the man, so how could she? What she did trust were her instincts. That little voice from deep inside that had been nagging her since Gaston first turned into this seductive piece of undead man meat couldn't be ignored.

"I'm glad I had a spare room." Gaston stopped in front of a door and turned to her. "I'm usually booked this time of year, but I had a last-minute cancellation. Poor demon. I don't know what he did, but Satan called him back to hell ten minutes after he checked in." He opened the door and stepped inside, gesturing for her to enter.

"Worked out for us then, didn't it?" Her stomach flitted as she entered the room. A queen-size sleigh bed draped in a burgundy duvet stood against the far wall, and matching antique end tables occupied either side.

"It is as if fate had a hand in our meeting, though we could have done without the murder investigation." He smiled, but his fangs weren't extended.

"Tell me about it." She sank onto the edge of the bed and ran her hand across the soft fabric.

Gaston opened another door and flipped a light switch. "Your private bathroom is here. Towels and complimentary toiletries are in the cabinet."

"Thanks."

"Tomorrow night, we can return to your home to gather your things." He clasped his hands, his jaw tightening. "Or Sophie can take you. The choice is yours, of course."

She gazed at the duvet, searching for a loose thread to toy with, but the fabric was in perfect condition. Clasping her hands in her lap, she lifted her head to look into his eyes. "Why are you helping me?"

He slowly shrugged. "I believe in your innocence, and it's my fault you are in this cucumber brine." He paced toward the bed. "May I?"

She nodded, and he sat next to her. "I didn't want to get you involved in this at all. It was my friends, Ethan and Jane, who revealed your existence to the Council. They were trying to help."

"How did they know about me?"

He chuckled. "I am quite taken with you, Maeve. I'm afraid my excitement at meeting you caused me to reveal more about myself than I normally would. I told my friends about you; they told the Council; the Council insisted on bringing you in. I hope you can forgive me."

The ice blue of his irises was pale like a glacier, and she wondered what mysteries lay beneath the surface. It went against her very nature to trust a vampire, yet Gaston had been nothing but kind— aside from his bat biting her hand, but he had a good enough excuse for his behavior.

"Have we met before? You seem so familiar."

He smiled again, but sadness filled his eyes. "Perhaps in another life." He rose to his feet holding out his hand, and she instinctively placed hers in his palm...again. Good gravy, it was like her body was on autopilot with this guy.

He pressed his cool lips to the backs of her fingers, and her entire body buzzed. An unwelcome giggle bubbling from her chest replaced the sadness in his eyes with mirth. "My room is at the end of the hall. If you need anything at all, simply say my name. I will hear you."

"I thought vampires were dead to the world during daylight hours."

"Not those as old as I am. I require very little sleep." He turned a switch on the wall, and light-blocking shades slid over the windows.

Wait. They were just light blockers, right? "You're not locking me inside, are you?"

He regarded her for a moment as if pondering her question. "No, you are free to leave. However, should you choose to go, both of our heads will be placed on spikes in the coven house courtyard. Sleep well, dear Maeve." He left the room, closing the door behind him.

"Well, gee. When you put it that way." Not that she had planned on trying to escape. The vampires knew where she lived and worked. She wouldn't get very far. Besides, she'd take this soft bed at Hotel Transylvania over a cell—or a spike—any day.

She might as well take advantage of the accommodations, so she slipped off her clothes, folding them and laying them on the antique dresser before heading for the shower. The water pressure was perfect, beating just hard enough to loosen her muscles, but not so hard as to leave her bright red. The complimentary shampoo smelled of lavender and rosemary, and there were even two choices of toothbrush: regular and one with special bristles for fangs. Her canines only extended in bat form, so she opted for regular with a strip of mint toothpaste.

Steam wafted into the bedroom as she opened the door, and she padded across the plush rug to find a small porcelain saucer next to her clothes. A cream-colored card, folded in half like a tent, sat next to the bowl. She picked it up and read the elegant script, which looked like it had been written with a fountain pen:

Cow's blood.
In case your bat is thirsty.
~Gaston

WARMTH SPREAD THROUGH HER CHEST. "Well, isn't he thoughtful?"

EIGHT

When Maeve woke the next evening, Gaston was already up, busying himself with domestic duties. He'd filled a large urn with blood for his vampire guests, and he'd cooked breakfast for the other nocturnal lodgers, which made sense. He did run a bed and breakfast, but she never expected a vampire to make the best eggs benedict she'd ever eaten. The man was full of surprises.

Addy had packed her a bag and dropped it off with the day staff, and by the time Maeve had stuffed her face and changed her clothes, Sophie had arrived to take her to the morgue.

Now, she sat in a plastic chair in the waiting room. White speckled linoleum lined the floor, and fluorescent lights hummed from above, casting a greenish glow in the sterile space. Most businesses had long since replaced this type of lighting with LEDs, but she doubted the dead complained.

Or hell, maybe they did. She was about to witness a corpse being brought back to life.

Sophie sat next to her and patted her shoulder. "I was nervous the first time too. Dead bodies make some disgusting sloshing sounds, and the eyes don't always move in unison, but Jasmine is quick. She knows how to get the information we need, and then she'll send him on his way."

She rubbed her tongue against the roof of her dry mouth. Why did it taste like she'd swallowed a handful of cat litter? "How is she going to bring him back without a body?"

"That's why we're at the morgue. I mean...it's also because she works here, but she can put a spirit into any dead body she wants. She put my grandma, who died in her twenties, into an old lady's body. It was weird as all get-out, but it worked."

"Sounds like fun."

"Trace and Gaston are on their way with something of Rene's. We'll all be there, and if he gets ornery, Jasmine can yank his spirit out of the body faster than a jackrabbit can get it on with a tree trunk. It's completely safe."

Maeve wiped her palms on her jeans. "They've been gone for a while. What if they can't find anything that belonged to him?"

Before Sophie could answer, the center of the waiting room shimmered. Then a massive hole opened like someone pulled down the zipper on a giant pair of pants, and Gaston, Trace, and a tall man with blond hair and skin even paler than a vampire stepped through. The moment they all set foot on the linoleum, the crack in reality slammed shut, and everything appeared normal.

Maeve gaped, and Trace grinned. "That never gets old. First time seeing a portal?"

"Yeah. Are you...?" She squinted at the man, trying to read his aura, but all she saw was nothingness. Like a void, but not one that would suck you into it. "Are you a demon?"

"Not exactly." He clicked a pen, and it transformed into a wicked scythe.

Trace clapped him on the back. "This is Death, but you can call him Asher. He's Jasmine's husband."

"When Jazz found out she'd be reanimating a vampire, she asked me to come." He turned the scythe back into a pen, stuffed it into his pocket, and held out his hand to shake. "Nice to meet you, Maeve."

She hesitated to take his hand. He was Death, after all, but Trace seemed okay after touching him. Holding her breath, she rose to her feet and shook. *Whew.* She exhaled. "Hi. Thank you for your help."

"Any time."

Gaston grinned at her and clutched a worn magazine in his hands. His smile made her stomach flutter again, but his fangs still didn't extend. She'd heard vampires had a hard time keeping them in check when they were attracted to someone. Gaston was either a master or the spark she felt every time he looked at her wasn't reciprocated.

Not that it mattered. She shouldn't have felt anything for the man.

The double doors leading deeper into the building swung open, and the necromancer stepped into the lobby. She wore a white lab coat, and her dark brown hair was tied back in a twist. "Sorry about that, guys. I hate being late for my appointments, but that last one was a doozy. Believe me, you didn't want to see what came out of him. You have something that belonged to the deceased?"

"We brought a pornography magazine from the

collection we found in his living room. This one appeared the most often perused."

Jasmine's lip curled. "Seriously? That's the best you could do?"

"You did say the more important the item to him, the better." Gaston moved toward her, and she took a step backward.

Reaching into her pocket, she pulled out a white cloth and wrapped it around the periodical, holding it like it might bite her. "Are any of the pages stuck together?"

"Probably," Gaston said before winking at Maeve.

Her lips curved upward involuntarily, and her stomach tightened, the flitting sensation making her feel like a schoolgirl getting noticed by her first crush. Gaston was not her first crush. He wasn't even *a* crush. He was just a man she found attractive. Someone she was unnaturally drawn to. Or maybe it was natural. So natural it came from deep inside her.

Gah! Stop ogling the man!

"Right. You can wait out here," Jasmine said. "One vamp in the room is enough for me."

Gaston's eyes constricted, and his fangs showed as he spoke. "I will not harm you, dear Jasmine."

Maeve's jaw clenched, something akin to jealousy churning in her gut. Why could he control his fangs around her but not around this married woman?

Wait. Why did she care? It wasn't like she wanted him to bite her. She never wanted a vampire's fangs anywhere near her flesh, but he wasn't even tempted. Was something wrong with her blood? Maybe the little taste he got in bat form was enough to turn him off.

"I'm not afraid of you," Jasmine's voice pulled her from her ridiculous thoughts. "I just don't like vampires. No offense."

"I'm afraid the feeling isn't mutual. I am also afraid Rene will refuse to talk to any of you. The vampires on the Council are elitists at best."

"He has a point, *cher*," Asher said. "You might get the information out of him faster if you let Gaston ask.

"I promise to behave myself." There he was with those fangs again.

And there *she* was, caring. *Damnit, Maeve. Get over it.* She moved next to him, close enough for her shoulder to brush his arm. "I'll keep him in line."

Gaston inhaled as if coming out of a trance. His fangs retracted, his pupils returning to their normal shape as he focused on her. Why did he have to be so devil-damned attractive? Her weight shifted, her body threatening to rise onto her toes and see if she couldn't get his fangs to come back out...with her tongue.

Instead, she pulled herself together like the confident woman she was and reminded him, "My life depends on this."

He rewarded her with a sexy smirk. "Indeed it does, *ma chère*."

Jasmine rolled her eyes. "Oh, fine. Stay across the table from me at all times."

"You have my word."

"Come on." Jasmine led them down a wide hall-way. Several closed doors lined the corridor, and she pressed her badge against a metal plate on the wall, unlocking one of them. "Welcome to the meat library."

Maeve wrinkled her nose at the smell of bleach and decay. She couldn't imagine working in a place like this. Her enhanced shifter sense of smell made the odor almost unbearable. Must be nice for vampires to just stop breathing when the air turned foul.

"Here." Sophie handed her a bottle of lavender oil. "Put some under your nose, and it'll help with the smell."

Maeve did as she was told, and it helped a little. Not enough to make her feel like she stood in a spring meadow, but enough to keep her from gagging. For now.

Jasmine set the magazine on a table and looked at Gaston from across the room. "Any preference on a body?"

"Someone old and decrepit would suit him," Gaston said.

The necromancer typed on a keyboard and scanned a list on the screen. "Huh. We don't have any elderly on the slabs. That's a first."

"Pity," Gaston said. "I suppose anyone will do."

"Nobody likes this guy, right?" Jasmine strode to a locker and opened the latch.

"He was a pretentious penis head who hated women and loved seeing his brethren staked."

"Cool. Let's bring him back as a woman." She slid out the drawer and uncovered the corpse.

Maeve pressed her lips together and peered at the dead person. She had dirty blonde hair and a halter top tan line. "How did she die?"

"Drug deal gone wrong. She was a meth head, got into it with the wrong person, gunshot wound to the chest." Jasmine gestured to the hole above the woman's left breast.

"She will do." Gaston moved closer to Maeve and rested a hand on the small of her back. "If this is too much for you, Sophie can take you outside."

"I'm fine." She moved away from his touch, not because his words offended her, but because the comforting gesture made her feel things she shouldn't be feeling for a vampire...especially when they stood in the morgue in front of a dead body.

"Let's do it then." Jasmine grabbed a dry-erase marker and drew some symbols on the metal table. Then, with one hand on the magazine, the other on the dead woman's head, she chanted something in a foreign language. The air thickened around them, and goosebumps rose on Maeve's arms in response to the electricity building in the atmosphere.

Gaston closed his eyes, becoming so utterly still he could have been a statue, and Maeve clutched his arm. She didn't mean to grab ahold of him. It was instinct. Honestly, it was, but it felt so good to be touching him. Like she'd been missing the feel of the sinew beneath his skin all her life, and she never knew it until this moment. He rested his hand on top of hers, and she inched even closer.

Yeah, there was definitely something wrong with her.

Jasmine pressed her hands together and bowed at the symbols she'd drawn. "It's showtime!"

The dead woman's eyes flew open, and one rolled toward Jasmine before the other followed. The corpse's head turned, the sound of crunching bones and sloshing fluid making Maeve's stomach lurch.

"Trash can is over there, if you need it." Jasmine nodded to the bin against the wall, and Maeve shook her head. She would not lose her breakfast over this. She'd seen a dead body before. Many of them. And, hey. At least her mind was back in the moment, right?

"What...?" The corpse spoke, the voice rough and raspy. "How did I get here? What sorcery did you use to subdue me, witch?"

"Not a witch," Jasmine said. "You're dead, and you need to tell us who killed you."

"How dare you, woman?" Disdain dripped from the last word, and he hissed at Jasmine, probably trying to bare his fangs, but the corpse's teeth had rotted from the drugs.

Jasmine sighed. "Gaston, do your thing."

Gaston moved closer, preparing to speak when

the corpse flung one arm toward Jasmine. It rolled onto its side before pushing upright and lunging off the table. Before Maeve could blink, Asher transformed into a seven-foot-tall skeleton in black robes and pointed his scythe at the corpse. "Back on the table, or I'll drag you to the tarpits and let you spend eternity there."

"Whoa." Maeve tightened her grip on Gaston's arm, her blood flushing cold. Was *that* what guided her family to the other side? Her churning stomach twisted.

"He only uses his skeletal form when necessary," Gaston whispered, as if reading her mind...which he probably could. She would have to find out if vampires had that ability when this was done.

The corpse clutched the table and sank onto the surface. "I remember you."

"You should." Asher returned to his human form, but he didn't put away his scythe. "I took you to the Underworld."

Rene brought his hands to his mouth. "Where are my fangs? My teeth!" he wailed. "What have you done to me? I had my fangs in hell!"

"Relax, Rene," Gaston said. "This body is not yours."

"Gaston Bellevue," he growled and turned

toward them with an icky, slopping, creaking sound. "You should be the one rotting in hell. You're lucky I met my demise before I could report your insolence."

Gaston chuckled. "Indeed I am. Who killed you?"

"Why should I tell you?"

"So we can bring your killer to justice," Maeve said, her voice sounding way more confident than she felt...sounding way more everything than she felt because the way one of the corpse's eyes drooped while the other rolled upward made a lot more than bile creep up the back of her throat.

Rene laughed, and the bullet wound dilated, a puff of air squirting out before some sort of yellow goo oozed from the opening. That was all it took for Maeve to lose it. She lunged for the trash can and hurled, and Satan have mercy, eggs benedict did not taste good the second time around. She heaved again and then clamped her mouth shut. She had to get it together. Gaston cut his gaze between the corpse and her while she attempted to swallow what was trying to come up.

"I'm okay," she muttered.

"Are you sure?" Sophie asked.

Maeve nodded and made the mistake of looking

at the body. Its eyes crossed before one rolled up, the other to the side.

She tried to hold it in. She really did, but her knees buckled, and her stomach heaved, the force so hard, it came out both ends. A massive fart that sounded like a trombone and smelled worse than the devil's dumpster exited her rear end at the same time as her breakfast splashed up from the bin and coated her shirt.

On her hands and knees, she coughed and then hurled again until every last bit of acidy, partially digested food was expelled along with her dignity.

Her ears burned, the heat spreading across her face, no doubt turning her blood red with humiliation. She hardly knew any of these people, and she'd just puked her guts out and stunk up the already rancid room in front of them. In front of *Gaston*.

Oh, the humiliation.

She could never recover from this. If the Devil rose up and offered to take her to hell right now, she'd gladly accept the invitation. Anything to get away from the embarrassment.

She wiped her mouth with the back of her hand and shot to her feet before darting out the door. Shouts sounded from behind her, and she gave herself half a second to turn around and look through the window next to the jamb. Gaston grabbed the corpse, slammed it down on the table, letting out a wicked hiss, and Maeve spun to continue her trek through the lobby and out the front door.

Damnit. She'd ridden here with Sophie. She briefly considered shifting and flying away, but she couldn't do that for three reasons. One: The whole having her head served up on a spike in the coven house courtyard issue. Of course, she could have flown to Bellevue Manor, but that led to issue two: She'd be naked when she got there, and she doubted a vampire would chance leaving any windows cracked for her to slip inside. If they stayed open in the daytime, sunlight leaking in might toast their buns a little more than they'd appreciate. And three: Sophie followed her into the parking lot while she was contemplating her escape.

"How ya feeling, hon?" She handed her a water bottle, and Maeve accepted it, swishing and spitting in the grass before taking a long drink to shove the sourness back into her stomach where it belonged.

"Physically, I'm fine. Emotionally...the stink bomb that shot out my ass made sure I'll never be the same again."

She gave her a sympathetic look and a tissue. "It

wasn't *that* bad. With all the commotion, I bet no one else noticed."

Maeve laughed dryly. "You had lavender oil under your nose. Imagine what Gaston smelled, what he thinks about me now. Gah!" She wet the tissue and tried to wipe her breakfast from her shirt. All she managed to do was smear it.

"Want a mint?" Sophie offered her a box of Altoids.

She took three. "Thanks. Would you mind taking me back to the B and B?"

Sophie hit the key fob, unlocking the car, and Maeve slid into the passenger seat. Sophie climbed in and started the car. "Gaston doesn't think any less of you, believe me."

Maeve scoffed. "Right. He told you that while he was slamming the reanimated corpse onto the table and hissing at it?"

She pulled onto the road and headed toward the Garden District. "No, but I do know how he feels about you."

"And how does he feel?"

"Let's just say he's a bit smitten." She smiled knowingly, though what exactly she could have known, Maeve wasn't sure. She'd only met Gaston a few days ago.

Still, the corners of her mouth twitched. If she were honest, she'd admit she was a bit smitten with him. "I bet he's not anymore. I humiliated myself."

"Oh, come on. We've all done embarrassing things. When I met Ethan, I threw up on his shoes. The second time I met Trace, I threatened to beat him with a vibrator."

Maeve laughed. "Seriously?"

"In my defense, he was naked in my apartment, and I thought the vibrator was a can of pepper spray."

"Oh, boy."

Sophie nodded. "Jane used to faint at the sight of blood."

"But she's a vampire."

"Uh-huh. And Gaston is a gentleman, believe it or not. He probably won't even mention it."

"But he'll know. I don't have a clue why I care. I should be livid with him. If he hadn't shown up at my sanctuary, I wouldn't be in this situation."

They stopped at a light, and Sophie looked at her. "But you do care."

She sighed. "Yeah, I do. He's too damn handsome for his own good."

Sophie curled her lip. "Not really my type, but I can see the appeal. He does have a mysterious air about him, doesn't he? Almost feels like you've known him forever?" She arched a brow.

"That's exactly how it feels." Maeve dragged her hands down her face. "Do you think he got the corpse to tell him who the killer is?"

"If Rene knows who killed him, they'll get it out of him." She pulled in front of Bellevue Manor and killed the engine.

"Good." Maeve unbuckled her seatbelt. "In the meantime, I'm going to wallow in self-pity in the tub."

Sophie patted her knee. "No problem. I'll be downstairs if you need me."

CHAPTER

NINE

Gaston sat silently in the passenger seat as Trace drove to the B and B. Maeve had lost control of her bodily functions during the resurrection, which wasn't surprising. She wasn't the first shifter to chuck up her cookies in Jasmine's presence, and she wouldn't be the last. Something about necromancy disturbed the living, while it had no such effect on the undead.

Sophie's car sat in front of the mansion, and Trace pulled into the drive. Worry over Maeve's condition had Gaston moving at vampire speed. He made it out of the car, through the revolving door, and into the living room before Trace could even unbuckle his seatbelt.

"Where's Maeve?" he asked Sophie.

"She's in her room." She cut her gaze toward the rotating door, and Trace stepped through to join them.

"How is she?" Gaston had wanted to run to her, to comfort her when she was sickened, but he'd focused on Rene instead, putting his goal of gaining information before Maeve's health. *Nothing* should come before a soulmate. It was a lesson he should have learned long ago.

"Embarrassed, but no worse for wear." Sophie waved a hand dismissively. "She'll recover. Did you get the information you needed?"

Trace nodded. "We have a video of Rene saying he thought it was a vampire with a facial scar. Sadly, he didn't get the chance to identify him before he was offed."

Gaston's jaw tightened. The councilman's description of the culprit did not bode well. "I'm not sure the Council will accept it as proof of Maeve's innocence, but we will try."

"Damn." Sophie's shoulders slumped. "I was hoping it was someone he knew."

"The slaying happened too fast for even a two-hundred-years-dead vampire to process it." Which meant the killer had to be much older than Rene. Probably older than Gaston as well.

"Okay. Well…" Sophie rose from the couch and took Trace's hand. "It was worth a shot. We'll give you some privacy with Maeve. Call us if you need anything."

"Thank you for your assistance." Gaston nodded, and Sophie and Trace slipped through the door.

His heart beat hard against his chest, a sensation he was growing accustomed to ever since he'd met Maeve. He ascended the stairs, fisting his hands and splaying his fingers as he approached her door. He lifted his arm to knock, but the sinking feeling in his stomach gave him pause. The killer might not have been someone Rene could identify, but Gaston had a feeling *he* could…and that Maeve probably could too.

He closed his eyes, finally daring to use his magic for the first time since the unsettling idea formed in his mind. Opening himself to the energy running through the city, he searched for the low vibration of the possible culprit. He found Ethan instantly, and Jane's energy, though weaker, registered in his senses as well.

Then it happened. The vim he was searching for clicked, and he recoiled, pulling his energy inward before the culpable vampire could sense him. It was as he suspected, and the news was not good.

The knob turned, and Maeve cracked the door. "Are you going to stand in the hall all night, or do you want to come in?" She smiled hesitantly, glancing at his eyes before averting her gaze.

"I would be honored to join you."

She opened the door all the way, and he stepped inside. Her bed had been turned down, the sheets rustled, and she pulled the duvet back into place before sinking onto the mattress and patting the space next to her. "What did you find out?"

"First, I need to apologize. I focused my attention on the corpse when I should have comforted you in your time of need." He accepted her offer and sat on the bed.

She laughed dryly. "Comfort from you was the last thing I needed. That was humiliating."

"Nonsense. It happens to many the first time they watch Jasmine work."

"Oh?" She gave him a skeptical look. "Did you puke in a garbage can and let out a massive stink bomb while you were at it?"

"Stink bomb? I'm not sure I understand what you mean." Yes, that was a lie. He might not have detected the odor, but he did indeed hear the melody emanating from her behind. He would spare her the embarrassment and insist he knew nothing, though. It was the least he could do.

"Yeah, right. Everyone smelled it."

"You forget that vampires don't need to breathe. I smelled nothing because I never inhaled unless I was speaking." That part was true. The overwhelming scent of bleach in the morgue would have singed his delicate nostrils if he had taken too many breaths.

"Oh." An adorable blush spread across her cheeks, and the scent of her blood blossomed beneath her skin. His fangs extended against his will, so he clamped his mouth shut, willing them into submission. With Maeve's aversion to vampires, he tried to appear as human as possible around her, which was no easy task. Her blood called to him like honey to the Pooh Bear Winnie.

"As for what Rene told us, I'm afraid I have bad news."

She flinched. "He didn't see the guy?"

"Not really. The killer moved too quickly. Rene went from undead to really dead before he even realized what was happening. He saw the bat transform, and he believes the killer was an old vampire."

"Fan-flapping-tastic." She lifted her arms and dropped them. "What now?"

Gaston took her hand, sandwiching it between both of his. She looked down at their entwined fingers and lifted her gaze to his eyes. When she didn't pull away, it took every ounce of willpower he could muster not to lean in and take her mouth with his.

"Did the man who murdered your colony have a facial scar?" He traced his finger from his temple, down the side of his cheek.

Her brow inched upward. "Yes..."

Gaston closed his eyes for a long blink. He couldn't deny it any longer. The evidence was too damning. "You were right. The killer is the same man who murdered your colony."

She gave her head a small shake. "I knew it. I knew I didn't run far enough away. He's here to finish the job...to drain me."

Gaston ground his teeth. That might not be the case. "Where did your colony live?"

"Florida. I should have kept flying all the way to California. That was my original plan, but I stopped at Wings of Love along the way. A witch ran the sanctuary back then, and she took me in. She cast a protection spell so no one would know I was there, and I got too comfortable."

She sucked in a shaky breath. "She passed away a few weeks ago, and when she died, the protection spell died too. Now the son of bitch has found me."

"It gets worse." *So* much worse. He scooted closer to her, his thigh resting against hers.

"What could possibly be worse than being hunted by a murderous vampire?"

"I don't think he wants to murder you. Not if he sticks to his pattern."

Her head snapped toward him, and she leaned away to look at him. "His pattern? What do you mean?"

Gaston inhaled deeply. Her sweet scent calmed his nerves.

She narrowed her eyes. "I thought you said you didn't breathe."

"I can when I want to. I like the way you smell."

Her cheeks reddened again. "Thanks?"

"The pleasure is mine, believe me. I'm going to tell you a story I have never shared with anyone else." Anyone besides Bridgette, but he would spare her that detail. It would only complicate things. "This may sound familiar to you."

"I'm listening."

"I told you before that I was raised by wolf shifters, did I not?"

She nodded.

"When I was human, we lived next door to a shifter family. They revealed their secret to me as I played with their litter frequently. When my parents died of the plague in 1653, they took me in and raised me as one of their own."

"Wow. You're old."

He chuckled. "Indeed I am. I lived with the shifters into my adulthood. That's when tragedy struck. A vampire killed the entire family, draining them all in one night. He saved me for last, and as he sank his fangs into my neck, I prepared to cross over to the Underworld."

Sadness expanded in his chest. He hadn't thought about this tragedy in many years. "He did not kill me. Instead, he turned me. Before the death sleep pulled me under, he removed the floorboards and dropped me beneath them. He put them back into place, and then I heard a horrible moaning. He screamed, and I assumed from the sound that the shifter magic had taken hold of him. Claws scratched at the floor, and a pained howl sliced through the night. Then silence."

A crease cut across her forehead, and compassion filled her eyes. "I'm so sorry, Gaston. I had no idea you were turned against your will. How terrible that must have been."

The ache in his chest stretched into his throat. "I awoke the following night alone and thirsty. I learned to fend for myself until he returned two weeks later and showed me his power. He had the ability to shift into more than a wolf. He could transform into a bear and a lion."

Maeve touched her fingers to her parted lips, and he could practically see the gears turning in her mind. "He'd done it before," she said.

"Twice."

"And he's still doing it. He's a serial killer." She closed her eyes and tipped her head back.

"He told me he always turns the last person so they can bear witness to his power. So his legacy can live forever." His fingers tightened around her hand. "Maeve, he doesn't want to kill you. He wants to turn you."

"Or, since I got away, he's pissed and wants me dead." She pulled from his grasp and shot to her feet. "I need to go home. I need my weapons. I have to kill the bastard."

"Olaf is five hundred years dead, and a vampire's power increases with time. It won't be an easy feat. I'm not even sure if I could defeat him alone."

"Yeah, well, his age won't matter when I unleash my wrath." She paced in front of the bed, fisting her hands and shaking her head adamantly. She was feisty and strong, and he admired her tenacity more than she could imagine. But she didn't stand a chance against a vampire as powerful as Olaf. No one did.

"Have you killed a vampire before?"

She stopped and faced him. "No, but there's a first time for everything."

"We must be rational about this." He rose and grasped her shoulders, trying to comfort her. "He took from me the same as he took from you. We are joined in our grief and in our need for vengeance, so we will figure out a way to destroy him together."

***

Maeve peered up at Gaston, and he looked back at her with conviction in his eyes. The fondness she felt toward him amplified, and the way he held her, his grasp firm yet gentle at the same time, sent a warm shiver down her spine. His presence calmed her, and his tragic story, so similar to her own, made her look at him in a different light. Maybe vampires weren't the monsters she'd made them out to be. Not all of them, anyway.

She swallowed the dryness from her throat. "You are nothing like I expected."

"What did you expect?" He squeezed her shoulders and released them.

She immediately missed his touch. "A pompous, self-important beast with no regard for humanity or concern for other supes."

"Ouch." He flinched. "That is quite a harsh judgment."

"Yeah, but you've proved me wrong."

"What do you think of me now?" He didn't move. She was certain his feet stayed firmly planted on the floor, but the energy between them shifted, making her feel as if he'd gotten closer.

She bit the inside of her cheek. His gaze was intense, the pale blue of his eyes deep like an abyss she could easily drown in if she wasn't careful. But she was tired of being careful with Gaston. "It doesn't make any sense, but I feel safe with you."

"I would never allow harm to come to you, Maeve." Her name sounded seductive coming from him. The deepness of his voice, the slight accent making him sound like he came from another time...

which he did. It was like he'd enveloped her name in promises that she couldn't wait to unwrap.

She licked her lips, and his gaze dipped to her mouth. *Oh, boy.* "I know. That's why I feel safe."

A sly grin tugged on one corner of his mouth. "What else do you think?"

She thought...she *knew* she was batshit crazy, but she couldn't fight his magnetic pull. She stepped toward him, slid a hand behind his neck, and pulled him into a kiss.

His lips felt cool against hers, not corpse-like as she'd expected, but more like how a peppermint makes your mouth feel when you suck on it. He slid his arms around her waist and tugged her against his body, and boy howdy, what a body it was. Everything about him was firm yet inviting.

He opened for her, and she slipped her tongue into his mouth to tangle with his. A sexy rumble emanated from his chest, and she lost herself in his embrace...until she accidentally licked his fang. The razor-sharp canine nicked her flesh, breaking the trance she'd succumbed to.

"Oh!" She pulled from his grasp, bringing her fingers to her mouth and touching the small puncture on her tongue.

"My apologies." Gaston covered his mouth, and

she smiled. She finally managed to make his fangs come out. "I try to keep them in check around you, but you surprised me. Are you okay?"

"I'm fine." She slipped out her tongue to show him. "Shifters are fast healers."

His brows drew together. "I hope this won't make you more averse to my kind."

"I'm starting to think my aversion may have been unfounded. You and your friends have been nothing but nice to me. Your Council is a bunch of pompous blowhards, but most governments are." She'd learned more about vampires in the past few days than she'd learned in her entire life. Still, she needed to pace herself. Focus on the issue at hand. She currently had a madman out to either kill her or turn her, and if he didn't get to her first, the vampire Council wanted to see her strung up like a bad Halloween decoration and burned at the stake.

Or maybe they wanted to behead her. Draw and quarter? "How does your Council usually execute shifters?"

"Don't think about that. They would have to get through me, and I could take them all on at once if need be. No one will lay a talon on you as long as I'm undead."

The voice in her soul, which didn't feel like nagging anymore, told her he meant every word.

She sank onto the bed and curled her legs beneath her. "So, Olaf. Won't the Council want to take care of him? I mean, he's a vampire killing in their territory. I'd think the Magistrate would want to exert control, right?"

Gaston sat on the edge of the bed next to her. "Once we convince them Olaf killed Rene and you are innocent, they certainly will. Sadly, the crimes against our families are out of their jurisdiction."

"One crime is enough, right? I mean, I'd love to see him fry like an extra-crispy undead chicken leg for what he did to my colony, but I suppose the reason doesn't matter...as long as the outcome is the same."

"He will be staked for his crimes."

"What are we waiting for, then? Let's go to the coven house and tell them."

Gaston shook his head. "The Magistrate is out of the country with his husband, and he is the only one who can hand down punishment. We will have to wait until he returns."

"Seriously? So I have to stay here and be babysat for the next three weeks because your ruler went on vacation?"

"Has your stay here been unpleasant?" Real concern pinched his brow, and she felt bad for how she made it sound.

"Not at all. The digs are great...way better than a prison cell."

"And the company?"

Her stomach fluttered. "The company has been nice too. I just hate sitting around when I know he's out there. What's going to stop him from killing someone else while he's looking for me? What if he tries to take out Trace's pack?"

"He can already shift into a wolf, so I believe they are safe. The local bobcat clowder, however... I will send word for all the area shifters to be on alert."

"And I guess I'm stuck inside until then." She sighed. At least Addy could run the sanctuary in her absence. Her day staff was used to managing without her, so unless there was a crisis, the bats would be fine.

"Not necessarily. Though it's been three hundred years, the sire/child bond is still present. I could sense Olaf's approach now that I know he's in the city."

Gaston's face tensed, and he pressed the side of his fist to his mouth like something was troubling him...which, duh, the man who murdered his adoptive family was in town. Of course he was troubled. "You could be right about Olaf wanting you dead. How did you escape him? He would have sensed your hiding place."

"I don't know. Maybe his gluttonous belly slowed him down. He was still chowing down on my cousin when I slipped out of the cabinet, shifted, and flew out the window. I guess by the time he was able to turn into a bat, I'd gotten far enough away."

He nodded solemnly. "Olaf is arrogant and proud. He would not take kindly to being bested by a shifter." He clasped his hands in his lap and stared at them for a good thirty seconds before he spoke again.

"I cannot bear to lose you a..." He pursed his lips. "If you could sense him, you would be safer. If he truly wants to turn you, we could take that option away from him."

"What do you mean?"

He angled his body toward her. "Allow me to turn you. If you are already a vampire, his hunt will cease if that is his game ending. If he wants to kill you, you will have heightened senses and speed."

"Turn me? Are you nuts-o?" Why in Satan's realm would he propose *that* as a solution to this problem? That wasn't a solution. It was another problem all on its own. "I'm not going to let you completely upend my entire life on a whim because another vampire *might* want to turn me. That's insane, Gaston." And there was only room for one crazy person in this B and B, and she already held the title.

His eyes flashed like he regretted the suggestion...or maybe he regretted her answer. "You are absolutely right. I don't know what came over me. Forget I even mentioned it." He stared straight ahead, his gaze seeming unfocused for a moment before he blinked and straightened his spine.

"Perhaps we should remedy the issue of you hardly knowing me."

Now that was a suggestion she could get on board with. She could think of plenty of ways she'd like to know him better, starting with what lay beneath his custom-tailored clothes. *Down, girl.*

"Morning has dawned, so I must retire for a few hours." He rose to his feet. "Tomorrow evening, let's meet in the garden, and you can ask me anything you want to know."

She grinned. "Anything?"

"For you, dear Maeve, I will be an open encyclopedia."

"I'll hold you to it."

His gaze smoldered. "I hope you do."

"I'm going to bring a list."

"I will tell you anything. Until then, good night, *ma chère.*" He bowed his head and headed for the door.

"Good night, Gaston."

The moment he left the room, Maeve grabbed her phone from the nightstand to send Addy a text: *Girl, you are not going to believe what just happened. Call me as soon as you wake up.*

She returned the phone to the charging station and snuggled under the covers with the biggest smile she'd felt on her lips in ages.

CHAPTER

TEN

The moment the sun completed its descent behind the horizon, Gaston walked out the back door and sat on a bench in the B and B garden. Wispy clouds stretched across the crescent moon, and the cool February air smelled of the sweet Taiwan cherry blossoms from the tree near the fountain.

Nerves had his stomach tied in unfamiliar knots. Any moment, Maeve would appear from the door to join him, and he both anticipated and dreaded her arrival. He wasn't used to feeling such uncertainty about a woman...hell, about anything.

After the way she kissed him last night, he *had* been certain she felt their bond. She'd leaned into him, such passion crossing from her lips to his, he'd nearly turned to a pile of ash. Even when he'd nicked her tongue with a fang, she had seemed pleased rather than horrified. And that tiny taste of her blood was sweeter than ambrosia.

But the mere suggestion of turning her had killed the moment faster than a guillotine on the Queen of Scots. The only way to keep Maeve safe and make her his for the rest of eternity would be for her to become a vampire...an idea she had rejected the moment the words crossed his lips.

He would have to woo her. To make her see him as more than the loathsome—yet incredibly hand-some—burden who had derailed her life.

The revolving door turned, and Maeve stepped through, wearing dark jeans with an emerald sweater that perfectly accented her hair's fiery hue. He rose and smoothed his midnight blue shirt down his stomach before bowing slightly—an old habit he'd never been able to break.

A glittering smile brightened her eyes. "Whenever you do that, you make me feel like an eighteenth-century princess."

"Yet you are a modern-day queen." He held out his hand, and much to his relief, she accepted the gesture, allowing him to kiss the backs of her fingers and guide her deeper into the gardens.

"Oh, please." She laughed. "Nobody worships me."

He did, and he'd be damned before letting her go another day without knowing. "A queen's purpose is not to be worshipped by her subjects but to serve them. You fulfill that purpose for the bats at your sanctuary."

Her smile widened. "Maeve O'Meara, Bat Queen. I like it."

They stepped into a wooden gazebo situated beneath a towering Magnolia tree and settled onto a bench. "I believe you intended to bring a list of questions to ask. Did your mind slip?"

"Oh, no. I've got them." She tapped her temple.

He chuckled. "Then ask away."

She narrowed her eyes, studying his, the movement of her mouth indicating she chewed the inside of her cheek. "Question one. Can vampires read minds?"

"Sadly, no." Though, he would love to know what thoughts tumbled through hers.

"Thank the devil." Her shoulders slumped in relief.

"You've had thoughts you don't want me to know about?"

"Plenty." She pressed her lips together, her eyes flashing briefly. "Sometimes it looks like you and your friends are having conversations in your minds."

"Yes, we have telepathy...or as Jane likes to call it...'thought speaking.' We can send our thoughts to another vampire's mind, but we can only hear another's thoughts if they send them to us."

"That explains why I wasn't hung up by my heels to bleed out when I met your Council."

"I'd have been staked long ago if they could read my mind." He angled toward her. "That was an easy one. What else would you like to know?"

"How long do vampires live? Or be undead?"

"Indefinitely, I suppose. We do not succumb to age or disease. In fact, as I mentioned yesterday, we become more powerful with time. As long as we don't have an accident or get killed, we'll go on in our undead states forever."

He pursed his lips. These questions weren't what he anticipated. She wasn't getting to know him at all, only vampires in general. "I expected your questions to be more personal in nature."

She ran her palms over her thighs. "I've got those too. I was just warming you up."

"I'm as warm as a corpse can be."

"Okay, then. Here goes…" She took a deep breath, straightening her spine and looking into his eyes. "How did you get your bat?"

"Ah, going straight for the vein, I see."

She lifted one shoulder. "It's the best way to get what you want."

"What do you want, Maeve?" When he said her name, she visibly shivered.

"I asked my question first."

"Indeed, you did." He rose and paced across the gazebo, where he pretended to inspect a vine of ivy climbing the trellis. How much to tell her? "The woman I loved long ago was a bat shifter…like you." He turned to look at her, and her throat bobbed as she swallowed.

"I never harmed her, I assure you. When I drank from her, the pleasure was mutual. Over time, her magic took hold in me, and I gained the ability to shift like her."

"Where is she now?"

Right in front of me. "She died more than one hundred years ago." He squared his stance, clasping his hands behind his back.

Her brow furrowed. "You said you loved her."

"Yes."

"So, why didn't you turn her so you could be together forever?"

He tried to keep his expression neutral. Considering her immediate rejection of the idea yesterday, the question surprised him. "I never got the chance. She was murdered on her way home from work."

"I'm so sorry. How awful that must have been." She stood and paced toward him, sliding her arms around his waist and resting her head on his chest. The warmth of her embrace soothed him, softening the pain of the memory.

"It nearly killed me." His voice caught in his throat, and he cleared it. "She was excited to learn when I felt the bat magic forming, said she couldn't wait to fly with me."

She pulled away just far enough to peer up at him.

"The first time I shifted was shortly before she died," he said. "I had planned to turn her that very night..." He kissed her forehead and gently pushed her away. "Enough of my tragic past." Though he longed to tell her the truth, that she was his long-lost love reincarnated, it was too soon. What if she rejected him? He couldn't bear to lose her a second time.

She looked at the gazebo floor for a moment before a sly smile curved her red lips. "If you don't mind a cheap imitation, I'd love to fly with you. My bat has been dying to stretch her wings."

His chest tightened, a wave of longing washing over him. He never dreamed he'd have this chance. "There is nothing cheap about you, dear Maeve, and I would be honored to join you in flight." More honored than she could imagine.

"Is it safe? I mean, with Olaf in town and everything?"

He closed his eyes and activated his magic, searching the ether for his sire's vibration. He sensed him nearly one hundred miles east, no doubt lying low after murdering a councilman. Gaston drew his energy inward, cutting off the connection. Olaf most likely felt nothing more than a tickle to his senses. As long as they stayed west, they would be safe.

"No harm will come to you on my watch, *ma chère*." Satan would have a new soul to torture before Olaf got within spitting distance of Maeve; Gaston would make sure of it. "He is nowhere near us."

"Do you ever hunt in bat form? The cow's blood you've gotten for me has helped, but there's nothing like blood straight from the vein." She laughed. "In case you didn't know."

Even in bat form, he preferred the taste of humans, but he could take a sip or two from another mammal for her. Anything for Maeve. "We shouldn't venture too far from home, but the zoo is close by. Have you tried polar bear?"

She arched a brow. "I can't say that I have."

"Shall we?" He called on his magic and transformed into his bat before she could change her mind.

Maeve parked her hands on her hips. "I suppose I should just leave a pile of clothes here in the gazebo?"

Right. He'd forgotten about that. He shifted back into human form, his vampire magic returning his clothes to their proper place as he transformed. "Apologies. I let my excitement get before me."

"I'll head up to my room and fly out the window. Wait here." She pranced out of the gazebo, a little spring in her step as she darted across the lawn and disappeared into the house.

Gaston waited beneath her window, and when her silhouette filled the pane, he imagined her undressing, the way her supple body would feel beneath his touch. Memories tangled with dreams of things to come...oh, how he would make her come.

A small brown bat dove from the window, her leathery wings expanding just before she collided with his head. He smiled. "Are you challenging me?"

She swooped again, a gust of wind ruffling his hair as she flapped her wings, wordlessly answering his question before she took to the sky.

"The game is on, *ma chérie*." He clamped his mouth shut. That term of endearment hadn't crossed his lips since Bridgette passed away. It felt good to say it aloud again.

He shifted once more, following Maeve into the night. They soared over the grand mansions of the Garden District, past the St. Charles streetcar toward Audubon Park. Massive oak trees spread out across the property, many older than Gaston himself.

They flew side by side, swooping and soaring, spiraling and racing until they reached the zoo, and the flight was everything he had ever wished it would be. The only thing that would make the night better would be for Maeve to be a vampire as well, so he could speak into her mind to let her know how much fun he was having. More fun than he'd experienced in a century.

He spotted the resident polar bear sleeping in its enclosure, its white fur gleaming in the moonlight. Maeve landed soundlessly beside the animal, and Gaston watched from his upside-down perch in a nearby tree as she hopped onto its shoulder, her small body not creating enough pressure to wake it. With a deep inhale, she leaned down and sank her fangs into its flesh. She shook her fur as she drank, her wings spread wide on her mark to steady herself.

She was exquisite.

Simply watching her drink was all the satisfaction he needed, but when she paused to look up at him, a question in her eyes, he longed to join her. He flew down and landed next to her. His weight disturbed the bear, and it growled, rubbing its head against the ground before drifting back to sleep.

Maeve dug in again, drinking until her belly extended, her thirst satiated. Gaston managed two sips, but he imagined the sensation similar to attempting a feast of tofu when you're accustomed to rare filet mignon.

"Hey! Get out of here, you mangy mongrels!" A night watchman beat a metal bar against the enclosure, startling the bear, who roared, snapping its enormous maw at Maeve. "Spread your rabies somewhere else."

Maeve and Gaston shot upward, darting into the leafy canopy next to the cage. She clung to a branch, her rib cage expanding and contracting rapidly. He scanned her body but found no outward sign of injury. Inside, she was scared to death, and not the pleasant kind of death.

Mongrels? Mange? *Rabies...?* How dare a human insult them that way?

Gaston dropped from the tree, activating his glamour to shield him from the prying view of any cameras and returning to his vampire form before his feet touched the ground. "I'll have you know; I'm cleaner than a newborn baby's conscience."

"Holy mother..." Of the three Fs, when faced with an adversary such as Gaston, most men chose to fight, assuming he was human as well. A few...the intelligent ones...chose flight. This man, however, decided to freeze. His metal bar, the one thing he could have used as a weapon, clattered on the cobblestone, and a wet spot started on his crotch and quickly spread down the length of his right leg, giving a new way to answer the proverbial "How's it hanging?"

The stench of urine assaulted Gaston's senses, souring his original plan of making a meal out of the man before making an example. He glanced up at the tree, where Maeve watched him with wide eyes, and he sighed. It would be bottled blood for him tonight. He waved a hand in front of the man's face. "A sound startled you, and you wet yourself. You saw nothing."

He transformed into his bat and returned to the tree. Maeve took off the second he roosted next to her, so he followed her back to the manor. She zipped in through her half-open window, and he perched on the sill, giving her time to dress.

"Was that really necessary?" she called from inside.

Was she expecting him to answer? Surely, she realized he couldn't talk in bat form any better than she could.

"You can come in."

He peeked through the window and found her wearing the complimentary bathrobe tied loosely at her waist. The rest of her clothes lay in a stack on her dresser. *Satan's balls on a silver platter.* Seeing her in this state of undress stirred so many emotions in his soul. But she sounded irritated, so acting on the feelings was out of the question. Damn his libido.

After slipping through the window, he returned to his normal form and clasped his hands in front of his pants...just in case his dick decided to give her a salute. "Which part of the evening is in question?" he asked.

"That poor night watchman peed his pants!" She cinched the robe tighter, both sadly and thankfully pulling the top closed across her chest.

"He insulted and frightened you. I returned the favor." He had defended her. How could she be so displeased?

"He didn't frighten me. He thought we were regular bats, which can carry rabies. You didn't have to scare the piss out of him."

Gaston opened his mouth to respond and closed it again, confusion making his lips pucker. "I did not mistake your rapid breathing. Your fur stood on end."

She sighed heavily and leaned against the dresser. "Gaston, I'm a living bat. A polar bear nearly bit me in two. That's a normal response. Do you go around terrorizing every human who looks at you wrong?"

Oh, dear. She had interpreted his chivalry as arrogance. "I only meant to protect you."

"I don't need protection from humans." She

crossed her arms. "Were you planning to drink from him?"

"Had he not released the contents of his bladder into his trousers, yes. I would have used glamour; he wouldn't have been harmed."

She shook her head. "This was a bad idea. I don't... I need to think."

What was there to think about? "You were aware of the manner in which vampires feed. Nothing has changed."

"Yeah, but knowing and seeing are two different things. You know what happened last time I saw a vampire feed." A tendon in her neck protruded as she clenched her jaw.

"That is different, and you know it. You witnessed a mass murder. The simple act of feeding harms no one."

She dragged her hands down her face. "Okay, sure, but you've got to understand. It's been three hundred years since your family was killed. For me, it's only been fifteen. The wound is still fresh, and seeing you reminded me of him."

His heart sank, and he bowed his head. He could not think of anything that would cut deeper than being compared to his sire. "My apologies. I did not mean to trigger you."

She didn't have to say another word. The look on her face said it all. He was no longer welcome in her presence.

"I will be down the hall." He opened the door and slipped out of the room.

ELEVEN

"Thanks for taking me on a daytime excursion, Sophie." Maeve walked down Royal Street, sandwiched between Addy and her new friend. "It's against my nature to be out at noon, but apparently, it's the only time I'm safe these days."

"My pleasure," Sophie said. "That's one advantage we shifters have over vampires. We aren't allergic to the sun."

Addy yawned. "And daytime is the only time we can get you away from Gaston. That man is goo goo for you, girl."

Maeve held in a groan. She hadn't yet told them about her night flying with the sexy vampire. Or how she had avoided him the two nights after that. The last Addy had heard about was the kiss.

"How's it going with him?" Sophie flashed a knowing smile. What was it with her and these expressions that looked like she knew more than she was letting on?

"Right now, it's not."

"What?!" Addy shrieked. "But you said…"

"I know what I told you, but that was before I almost witnessed him drain a man." Okay, "drain" wasn't fair. He most likely would have taken a few sips and been on his way, but still. She hadn't been prepared to watch him feast on a human. Not yet.

"Really?" Addy yawned again. Maeve wasn't the only nocturnal shifter in the group.

"Hey, Soph? Is there somewhere we could stop for coffee? I'm afraid we'll be carrying Addy home if we don't get some caffeine in her."

"I know just the place." Sophie led them down the street to a three-story building painted light blue with white trim. *Evangeline's Coffee and Potions* was scrawled in a fun script over the door, and the decadent scents of cinnamon, vanilla, and coffee beans danced in the air as soon as they crossed the threshold.

"Welcome to Evangeline's," a woman with curly

black hair and an infectious smile greeted them. "Sophie!" She wiped her hands on a dishtowel and strode around the counter to pull Sophie into a tight hug. "It's been a minute. What have you been up to?"

Sophie laughed. "How much time have you got?"

"I don't have to be at the coven house until two. Let me make you gals some drinks, and we can head up to my apartment." She offered her hand first to Maeve and then to Addy. "I'm Crimson."

Maeve blinked. "High Priestess Crimson?"

"That's me."

"Wow. I've heard your story. You took going to Hell and back to a whole new level." She shook her head. "I'm Maeve, and this is Addy."

"Nice to meet you. I've heard about your story too." Another knowing smile. Had Gaston told them something? He was the only other person she'd spoken to since the ordeal began.

"Have a seat, and I'll whip us up something warm. My treat." Crimson sauntered around the counter and began turning knobs, grinding beans, and making steam. The delectable scent of coffee increased tenfold, and as she poured the frothy milk into the cups, Maeve's mouth watered.

"I didn't think you were serious when you said you were friends with the High Priestess," Addy whispered.

"Oh, yeah. We've got history." Sophie laughed. "I'll tell you about it sometime."

"Cinder," Crimson called into the back of the shop, and a woman with stark white hair streaked with hot pink strode out. "Can you woman the fort for a while? I've got some catching up to do."

"Of course, High Priestess." She gave a little curtsey.

"If you don't start calling me Crimson, I'm going to turn you into a wombat. Save the titles for the coven, mmkay?"

"Yes, ma'am."

Crimson rolled her eyes, but her smile showed her affection for the young woman. She set four steaming cups of coffee on a tray and jerked her head to the back of the shop. "C'mon up."

Maeve and her friends followed the High Priestess up two flights of stairs. She started for the doorknob since Crimson's hands were full, but the witch muttered something under her breath, and the lock disengaged, the door swinging open to reveal a loft apartment filled with oil paintings.

"Wow." Maeve turned a circle in the entry, taking it all in. "You're an artist too?"

"Sure am. Come. Sit." She settled on a white sofa and set the tray on the coffee table. Sophie sank next to her, and Maeve and Addy took the two accent chairs on either side.

After Crimson handed them their drinks, Addy squared her shoulders at Maeve. "Okay, spill it. You can't tell me you made out with a sexy vampire and then leave me thinking you've got a new beau for three days. What happened?"

Maeve sipped her coffee. Sweet notes of vanilla and nutmeg tamed the bitter chicory, the milk giving it a smooth finish that felt like velvet sliding down her throat. "This is the best coffee I've ever tasted. Is there magic in it?"

"Only the magic of caffeine and sugar," Crimson said. "My mother perfected the blend."

"Don't change the subject." Addy leaned her elbows on her knees. "What's going on with Mr. Tall, Pale, and Sexy? Don't you like him?"

"I do. That's the problem."

Sophie tilted her head. "Why is that a problem?"

"Because he's a *vampire.*"

Crimson arched a brow. "I was raised by earthbound angels, yet I married a demon. Stranger matches have been made."

Sophie leaned over to pat Maeve's knee. "Tell us what happened, hon. Maybe we can help you work through your reservations."

She let out a dry laugh. "What is this? Group therapy?"

Sophie screwed her mouth over to one side. "It could be. Hold that thought." She pulled her phone from her pocket and typed on the screen. A moment later, a loud whack echoed through the hallway outside, and a painting fell from the wall after whatever it was made impact.

"Son of a reaper!" A sultry voice said through the door. "A warning this place was portal-proof would have been nice."

Crimson shook her head and strode across the room to open the door. "I'm the High Priestess, Katrina. Did you really think you could just pop into my apartment?"

Katrina's eyes flashed red—demon red—before she strutted past the witch. Another demon followed her in—a man with dark brown hair and a chiseled jawline. He sat in the last available chair, and Katrina perched on the arm.

"Sophie said it was urgent, so I assumed you'd

let down the barrier." She pulled her long brown hair over to one side.

Sophie winced. "Sorry about that. Anyway, you're familiar with Maeve's story, right? With Gaston?"

The demon's gaze slid down Maeve's body before returning to her eyes. "You're gorgeous. I see why he likes you."

"Umm…" Maeve's stomach fluttered, and heat pooled in her core. *What the hell?* First of all, was there a single supe in New Orleans who *didn't* know her story? And second, why was she suddenly all hot and bothered in a room full of women?

"Katrina is a succubus. Gabe is an incubus." Crimson returned to her spot on the couch. "Go easy on her, will you?"

That explained a lot.

"Sorry." Katrina crossed her legs, and the strange sensations in Maeve's body ceased. "How can I help?"

She held up her hands. "Whoa, y'all. I don't think this is what I need. If I want to get it on with Gaston, I won't need any help."

"Gah." Sophie flipped her hair behind her shoulder. "I should have explained. Katrina and Gabe are sex and love therapists. I thought having profes-

sionals here might help you figure out your reservations."

Maeve covered her face with her hands and squeezed her eyes shut. She did not want to discuss her emotions with five other people when she couldn't even figure out how she felt herself. Then again, two therapists, her bestie, a witch, and a wolf shifter might be exactly what she needed to help figure all this out. She sure as hell wasn't making any progress on her own.

"Tell us what's going on," Gabe said.

She let out a slow breath. "I like Gaston. I really do, but..."

"Start with the kiss," Addy said. "Who made the first move?"

She drew her shoulders toward her ears. "I guess I did. The chemistry between us was hotter than hellfire, so I went for it."

Sophie scrunched her nose. "How was it with the fangs and all?"

"It was nice." Her mind flashed back to the kiss, and she couldn't fight her grin.

"Maeve..." Addy scolded. Her bestie expected a real answer, so she might as well be honest.

"It was magnificent, okay? And his fangs... He nicked my tongue accidentally, and I... I liked it. My reaction surprised me. All this time, I thought I hated vampires, but it turns out I only hate the one."

Katrina watched her silently, but Addy was on the edge of her chair. "Then what happened? Why are you holding back?"

"I freaked out the next night. We were out flying, and a night watchman at the zoo caught us in bat form drinking from a polar bear. Gaston got all territorial and scared the piss out of the guy. Literally."

Sophie laughed. "That sounds like Gaston. He's a character. I'm sure he glamoured him before he drank."

"He didn't drink from him. I think it was partly because the guy peed his pants and partly because he saw me watching. I'm not sure what I would have done if I'd actually seen him drink."

Gabe rested his hand on Katrina's knee. "I thought you were a vampire bat shifter."

"I am."

"Then you were already aware of how vampires feed." Katrina gave her an *I don't see what the problem is* look.

"Yes, I know. It's just so weird with Gaston. And the day before that, he suggested I let him turn me into a vampire to protect me from Olaf. It was too much, you know? I'm still adjusting to all this."

"Who's Olaf?" Addy asked.

"He's the killer," Crimson said.

"And Gaston's sire, which makes this even weirder." Maeve shook her head. "I can't be a vampire."

"Why not?" Sophie asked. "I get not being down with cold and clammy for eternity, but if you're going to be with Gaston, you'll have to get used to it. Jane says you can't even feel the cold when you're the same temperature."

"And you already drink blood, right?" Crimson asked.

Maeve blew out an exasperated huff. "Animal blood and only in bat form."

"You're already nocturnal," Addy said. "Your life wouldn't change all that much. Plus, you'd get super-strength, even better senses, and immortality."

"And glamour," Sophie added. "I'd give my left tit to have those mind control powers."

Maeve pursed her lips. They all had valid points, but still... "I hardly know him."

Katrina cocked her head. "That's an odd thing for a reincarnated soulmate to say. I doubt he's changed much in the hundred or so years you've been gone."

Her brows scrunched until her forehead ached. Reincarnated soulmate? "What are you talking about?"

Sophie's eyes widened, and she looked at Crimson, whose mouth dropped open.

Katrina smiled slyly. "He hasn't told you."

"Oh, shit." Gabe rubbed his temple.

"Maeve?" Addy looked at the women before focusing on her. "What are they talking about?"

All the blood in her head rushed down to her stomach, sinking it into her shoes. The woman he loved...the bat shifter. The night he transformed in the sanctuary... "Oh my gods. Bridgette."

"So, he *did* tell you?" Sophie bit her bottom lip. "Please say he already told you, and we didn't just spill the beans, mash them up, and serve them to you in a burrito."

"Maeve?" Addy asked again.

"He thinks I'm his long-lost love." She turned to the women on the couch. "And he told everyone this? Everyone except me?"

Sophie slapped her forehead. "Oh, shit. He's going to kill us."

Her head spun, her thoughts racing a thousand

miles a minute. "Why? Why does he think that? Just because I'm the only bat shifter left in Louisiana, it doesn't mean I'm the one he loved a hundred years ago."

"He's got a picture of her," Sophie said. "She looks exactly like you."

Maeve shook her head. "It's got to be a coincidence. How is that even possible? Souls go to the Underworld when people die."

"And some get another chance at life," Crimson said. "Like you."

"Wow," Addy said dreamily. "No wonder you hit it off with him. You're soulmates."

She clutched her head. "I don't. I can't believe it."

"I can give you proof if you want," Crimson said. "All I need is a strand of your hair, and I can cast a spell to find out."

"I'm not sure I want to know." It would explain so much if it were true, though. The magnetism between them. Her trust in him. The reason her heart kept insisting she apologize for freaking out on him even though her stupid brain wanted her to steer clear because of something that happened fifteen years ago.

"Do it, Maeve," Addy said. "You have to find

out."

The room spun. The blood pooling in her feet hadn't yet returned to the parts of her body that needed it, and if her heart didn't stop beating like a jackhammer, she might pass out from shock.

"Can someone get her a glass of water and a cold compress before we have to clean whatever it is bat shifters eat from Crimson's rug?" Katrina asked.

"Here." Sophie crouched in front of her and handed her a glass. "Take a drink and a deep breath. I know it's a lot to wrap your mind around."

No kidding. Maeve sucked in a deep breath, held it for a couple of seconds, and then let it out slowly. She sipped the water, focusing on the cooling sensation sliding down her throat. Another deep breath. Another sip of water. The room slowed its spin, the dizziness subsiding. "Thanks," she croaked.

"Are you okay?" Addy asked.

"Yeah. I'm fine." She downed the rest of the water and set the empty glass on a coaster before looking at Crimson. "Tell me about this spell."

The witch rose and strode into the kitchen. "I'll mix up a potion and chant the incantation, and it'll give me a glimpse into your past lives if you have any."

"What do I have to do?"

"Yank out a single strand of hair. It has to include the root for the reading to be accurate." She gathered jars and bundles of herbs from her cabinets and set a large copper bowl on the counter.

Sweet Cerberus, was she really going to do this? "Are you sure it will work? It won't give any false positives, will it?"

Crimson laughed. "It's not a pregnancy test."

"She channels the goddess," Sophie said. "Her spells always work these days."

Maeve flashed a questioning look. "These days?"

"Mm-hmm," Sophie hummed through tight lips.

"Yeah. Okay, let's do it." She grabbed a lock of hair and yanked. Sharp pain sliced through her scalp where the hairs came free, and she carried the strands to the kitchen.

"Jeez, that's like ten. I only needed one." Crimson swept them into her palm. "Give me a few minutes to mix this up."

The first liquid she poured made the room smell like lavender. Next was lemon, and then jasmine. She crushed a spicy herb with a mortar and pestle and poured it into the concoction. "Herbs and lemon, joy and strife. Take me back to her previous life."

She picked up the hairs and dropped them into the bowl. The second they touched the potion, the liquid hissed, and a stream of purple smoke rose into Crimson's nostrils. Her lids fluttered shut, and she swayed on her feet.

A minute passed. Then another. Maeve and her friends watched Crimson in silence, time seeming to halt and stretch on forever in tandem. Finally, after what felt like an hour but had probably only been five minutes, Crimson smiled and opened her eyes.

"Gaston was right. You are his soulmate."

Of course she was. The moment Crimson confirmed it, Maeve felt it in her soul like she should have known it all along. Gaston knew from the moment he met her, though, and he never said a word. Irritation bubbled in her chest...or was it heartburn? She crossed her arms. It was definitely irritation. "Why the hell wouldn't he tell me something like that?"

TWELVE

"Are you sure you don't want to go hunting?" Trace lounged on the loveseat in Gaston's living room, watching *Friends* reruns.

"Yeah, old man," Ethan said from the adjacent sofa. "It's still Mardi Gras season. Don't tell me you've already gotten your fill of drunk tourists."

Gaston glowered at his closest friend. He hadn't had a drop of alcohol since Maeve came back into his life, and he would remain sober until he'd vanquished Olaf to the deepest pit in hell. He had to hold his wits close. "Tempting, but no, thank you. I'm not leaving the manor with Maeve alone upstairs."

"Sophie and I are happy to keep an eye on her if

you need to get out and stretch your wings," Trace said.

"I won't leave her, whether or not she wants me here. Not until her safety has been assured."

Ethan flashed a sympathetic look. "She's still not talking to you?"

He ground his teeth. "She went on a daytime excursion with Sophie and returned before I left my room. She's probably sleeping."

A look passed between Trace and Ethan that Gaston didn't care to interpret. Maeve would come around. He simply needed to give her space to process her emotions. Once she came to terms with the way he fed, then he would work on winning her heart. He would make her his in this life before sharing the knowledge that she was also his long ago.

Trace cracked his knuckles. "You still haven't told her, huh?"

Ethan chuckled. "He's too chicken."

A growl rumbled in Gaston's throat. "I am no form of poultry: turkey, pheasant, chicken, or otherwise. I have a plan. She must see that I love the woman she is today before she learns of my love for her in the past."

"That, and he's scared to death of rejection." Ethan shrugged.

"You forget your place, young one."

"Riiight. When's Mike going to get here so we can start the movie? Jane will make peanut butter of my nuts if I'm not home before dawn."

The door rotated, and the demon in question stepped through. "Relax. You know I can portal you home in a split second." Mike wore jeans with a maroon t-shirt, and he grabbed a can of Coke from the fridge before plopping onto the couch next to Ethan.

Trace picked up the remote, but before he could press Play, Mike held up a hand. "I was talking to Crimson before I portaled over. She hung out with your girl this afternoon."

His girl. He liked the sound of that. "I'm happy to hear she's fitting in with our group."

Mike rubbed his hands together. "You might have a problem with how well she's fitting in when you hear what happened."

Gaston looked at him, silently urging him to continue. He didn't take the hint.

"Are you going to brew the tea, or must I suck it from your veins?"

"It's *spill* the tea," Ethan said.

Gaston shot him a hard look, and he clamped his mouth shut.

"The girls didn't know you hadn't told Maeve about the whole reincarnation business."

If Gaston's blood behaved like a human's, he would have paled.

"And," the demon continued, "they might have accidentally let the hellcat out of the bag for you."

His nostrils flared out of habit, though he wasn't breathing. "Might have or have indeed?"

Mike lifted his hands, palms upward. "They told her. Then Crimson performed a spell to show her it was true. Sorry, man. Maeve knows."

Gaston leaned forward, dropping his head in his hands. This was not how the situation was supposed to play out. Now, not only was Maeve disgusted by his feeding process, but she was probably in shock from the news. No wonder she hadn't ventured downstairs this evening.

"Which one told her?" he asked through clenched teeth, his fangs extending fully.

Mike drummed his fingers on his knee. "Katrina made a casual comment, and it spiraled from there."

"Of course it was the succubus. I doubt it was an accident."

"You'll have to talk to the girls about that. I can only tell you what Crimson told me."

The sound of footsteps muffled by the hall runner sounded from above, and Gaston cast his gaze to the stairs. Sadly, Maeve did not appear, and a demon couple in formalwear descended the steps instead.

Gaston rose and bowed toward them. "Have a lovely evening."

"You too," they said in unison.

His evening so far was anything but lovely. "I must speak to her. Go ahead and begin the movie. I will watch it another time."

"Good luck," Ethan said in his mind as Gaston took the steps two at a time.

"Maeve?" He knocked lightly on her door. "May I come in, *ma chère*? We have things to discuss."

She didn't answer, so he pressed his ear against the wood, focusing on the sounds from within. A lone cricket chirped outside the window, and the sound of the breeze rustling the leaves in the courtyard filled the room.

"Maeve?" He knocked again, louder this time, but she still didn't answer. A thread of panic wove through his veins, turning them to ice. His mansion was portal-proof, yes, but the spell wouldn't stop an intruder from climbing the trellis and coming in through the window. Or from flying in...

Olaf.

Gaston jabbed his hand into his pocket and pulled out the master key. Sliding it into the lock, he gave it a twist and opened the door. The room stood empty. The bathroom door was ajar, so he threw it open, inspecting the tub behind the shower curtain.

Nothing.

He leaned out the open window, scanning the ground below for signs of an intruder. The garden remained undisturbed. "Maeve?" he shouted into the night. "Maeve, dear, are you there?"

No response.

"Satan's balls! She's gone!" If that murderous, traitorous bastard harmed a single tuft of fur...

He shot down the stairs faster than a hellbound ghost running from a reaper and headed straight for the fridge to fuel himself for a fight. A carafe of O Neg sat on the top shelf, and he grabbed it, chugging the contents without bothering to heat it up. He spun for the door, but Ethan, Mike, and Trace blocked his path.

"What's going on?" Ethan asked.

"Maeve is missing. Her window is open, and she's gone. I called out to her." He fisted his hands and stepped toward them, but they held their ground, refusing to budge. "Olaf has her; I must go after her."

"Slow down, old man." Ethan held up his hands. "Take a breath."

"I cannot breathe while her life is in peril. Move out of my way before I do the moving for you."

Trace widened his stance. "How do you know Olaf has her? Can you sense him?"

"I will as soon as I get out the door, and when I find him, I will tear his limbs from his body, impale him like the great Vlad Tempest himself, and rip off his head last so he can feel every bit of pain he has caused me."

Mike whistled. "Remind me not to get on Gaston's bad side."

"This is not a joke," he growled.

"Okay," Ethan said. "We'll help you go after him, but listen to me first."

Gaston glared.

"When you find him, don't demand to know where Maeve is, okay?"

"That is exactly what I will do."

"What if he doesn't have her? What if he doesn't have a clue that she's staying here and you go in with your fangs bared and claws out, tipping him off to her location?"

He opened his mouth to argue, but his friend had a point. What if Olaf didn't have her? But then... "Where else would she be? She knows leaving without an escort is grounds for immediate beheading."

"Maybe she snuck out with Sophie again," Trace said. "Let me call her and see."

Mike nodded. "She could have climbed out the window to avoid you. Crimson has done that a time or two."

Dear Satan, did she hate him so much that she would resort to such tactics? He had to find her and make things right.

"She's not with Sophie, but the girls are on their way over. They'll wait here in case she comes back."

Gaston nodded. Thank the devil he had good friends. "I will find Olaf and speak to him. I will not mention Maeve until I am sure he has her."

"Good plan," Mike said. "We've got your back if things get ugly."

Gaston led the way onto the front porch, where he could more easily locate Olaf and Mike could open a portal to take them to his location. Sophie's car skidded to a stop on the curb, and she, Jane, and Crimson piled out to join them.

"That was fast," Ethan said as they climbed the porch steps.

"Sophie drove like a bat out of hell to get here," Jane said. "No offense, Gaston."

"Give me a moment to locate Olaf, and we'll be on our way. Please contact me immediately if Maeve returns home on her own."

"I could do a quick scrying spell to see if I can locate her." Crimson held up a crystal pendulum. "If she's not with Olaf, it would save you the trouble of confronting him."

Gaston threw his hands in the air. "Would you all stop trying to talk me out of this? Olaf must be stopped, and he must be stopped now."

"There's no reasoning with him when he gets like this," Ethan said. "Let us know if you hear from her."

"I, for one, am ready for a fight." Jane gestured to her boots. "I've got my stiletto stakes on. The very ones I used to vanquish that twit constable way back when."

"Thank you, Jane. I appreciate your enthusiasm." Gaston closed his eyes and focused his energy while Crimson and Sophie slipped inside.

This time when he felt the low vibration of his sire, he didn't pull back. He let his own energy wash over him, which, in hindsight, wasn't the brightest thing to do. He'd just given Olaf a heads-up that he was looking for him. "We must move now. Mike, please take us to Lafayette Cemetery Number One."

"My pleasure." With a swipe of his arm, the demon tore a hole in reality. The edges of the rip burned bright red, and on the other side lay the city of the dead.

Gaston stepped through first, and the others followed before Mike closed the portal behind them. The cemetery took up the entire square block, and rows and rows of aboveground graves lined the space. A vampire usually felt a sense of peace surrounded by the dead, but a fist of dread squeezed Gaston's heart until he thought it would burst.

A parade a few streets over filled the air with music and revelry, making it impossible to locate Olaf by sound alone. "He is in the cemetery. Of that, I'm certain."

"Right." Jane nodded. "We'll fan out and find him."

"If you encounter him, do not engage. He is powerful and will not hesitate to rip your heads off."

They split up, Jane walking with Trace-in-wolf-form and Ethan accompanying Mike. Gaston crept along the outer wall alone, breathing deeply and searching the air for Maeve's scent. He couldn't sense her, which could either be good or very, *very* bad.

He paused by a crumbling grave. Years of neglect had caused the stucco to weather away, exposing the brick and mortar beneath. The top cover had broken, leaving the inside exposed, and Gaston peered into the opening. He would not have been surprised to find his sire hiding inside, waiting to attack, but the tomb stood empty.

"Gaston, we found him," Ethan thought-spoke. *"Three rows in. We'll hang back."*

"He will sense you and Jane. I want you to stand behind me and get all this on video. Tell Trace and Mike to stay out of sight."

"I got you, boo," Jane said. *"Let the filming begin."*

Gaston stalked toward the third row of tombs, and Jane caught up as he met Ethan. Forming a triangle of the undead, with Gaston at point, they stepped between the graves to face their maker.

Olaf kneeled over a lifeless body. His blond hair was shaved on the sides and braided down the middle, and he wore black leather from shoulders to boots. He lifted his head, and blood ran down his chin.

Flashing a sinister smile, he rose to his feet. "If I had known you were bringing guests, I would have brought enough to share."

"Olaf," he growled.

"Gaston." His sire wiped the blood from his face with a handkerchief and stuffed it into his inner jacket pocket. Cocking his head, he studied Ethan and then Jane. "What's this? A family reunion?"

Jane moved beside Gaston. "Murder is illegal here, even for vampires. You'll be staked for this."

Olaf tossed his head back and laughed. "I would like to see them try. Really, it would be fun to take out an entire coven." He tapped a finger against his lips. "Perhaps I should give it a go."

Jane started toward him, but Gaston held out his arm to block her. *"Do not be an imbecile. You are a fledgling."*

Jane let out a slow hiss and returned to her place by Ethan, keeping her camera trained on the ancient vampire.

Gaston held back a growl. He wanted to throttle his sire, to smack that smug grin off his face and demand he tell them where Maeve was. "What are you doing in New Orleans?" he asked instead.

Olaf touched his tongue to the tip of a fang. "I have unfinished business with a resident, though I have yet to decide if I'm going to turn her or kill her. After I'm finished, I may stay a while, now that I know I have family here. Perhaps you'll have a new sister soon."

Gaston bared his fangs and stormed toward his sire. "Where—"

"*Gaston, don't,*" Ethan said into his mind. "*We still don't know if he has her.*"

Olaf didn't budge from his spot. "Aren't you going to introduce me to my grandchildren, son?"

"I am not your son."

His sire laughed. "No? If memory serves, your other family died ages ago."

To hell with it. To hell with him. Gaston lunged, wrapping his arms around Olaf's shoulders and tackling him. They landed on the dead human with a *thunk*, and a fountain of blood squirted from the neck wound right into Gaston's eyes.

"Look at that," Olaf said. "I guess I didn't drain him after all."

Gaston sat up before rearing back and landing a punch square on his sire's jaw. He might as well have punched the side of a tomb. Olaf's face was as hard as concrete, and Gaston's knuckles split open to the bone. "What have you done?"

In a flash of ancient vampire speed, Olaf shoved Gaston and hauled him up by the front of his shirt before pinning him against a gleaming white mausoleum. Olaf's forearm pressed into Gaston's chest, rendering him immobile. "I've done plenty in my five hundred years. You'll have to be more specific."

"You murdered a councilman."

"He had the audacity to write me up. What else could I do?" He tilted his head. "What a pity one younger than you gained a seat on the Council before you. I did you a favor, son."

Ethan and Jane moved into position behind Olaf. *"Say the word, and we'll join the fight,"* he said.

"Not yet." The pressure on his rib cage made it impossible for him to draw in a breath. Without breath, the slew of curses he wanted to spout at his sire never made it past his throat. He would have to stoop lower than even he normally did.

Olaf leaned in, pressing harder, and Gaston did what any unrespectable vampire would do in this situation. He kneed him in the balls.

His sire grunted, loosening his grip enough for Gaston to get in another kick. This time he lifted his leg and rammed his shin into Olaf's nuts. He shoved him away, tension coiling in his muscles as he prepared to lash out.

Olaf adjusted his dick and had the gall to chuckle. "You've grown stronger, young one. I look forward to another match when you are better prepared. Now, I must continue my search." In a flash of magic, he turned into a bat and took to the sky.

Gaston called on his bat, but before he could transform, Jane's voice stopped him. "Maeve's at the B and B." She held up her phone. "Sophie and Crimson are with her."

His shoulders sagged in relief. "Mike," he called into the darkness, and the demon and the shifter appeared from behind a tomb. "Please take us home."

"Will do." He waved his arm, and a portal opened, Bellevue Manor standing on the other side. They stepped through onto the porch, and Gaston started for the door.

"Hang on a sec." Jane grabbed his arm. "You can't go in looking like you dove face-first into a pot of spaghetti sauce. Let me get you a towel."

She slipped through the door. A minute later, she returned with a wet washcloth and swiped it across his forehead. "The good news is, it sounds like Olaf doesn't know where Maeve is." She ran the cloth over his eyelids and down his cheek.

"Yes, I suppose that is a small morsel worth savoring."

Jane wiped the cloth down his neck and held up the red-marred fabric for him to see. "Handsome as ever. Now, go in there and win back your girl."

"He did what?" Maeve held a throw pillow against her chest, squeezing it tighter as Sophie filled her in. Gaston and his friends had gone after Olaf because he thought she had been captured. "Please tell me they're okay."

"I called Jane the second you came inside, so hopefully—" Her phone chimed, and she swiped the screen. "Yep. They're all good. On their way back now."

The tension in her chest partially released, but Satan have mercy; if anything had happened to them, she would've never forgiven herself. The rotating door spun, and a flash of *something*—a vampire maybe?—whizzed through to the kitchen and back outside.

The door spun again, more slowly this time, and Gaston stepped into the foyer. Maeve barely noticed his friends following him in; she was too busy fighting the urge to run and throw herself into his arms.

"Where were you, *ma chérie*? I was so worried." He approached her tentatively, and Sophie and Crimson, who had been sitting on either side of her, moved so he could join her. He sank down beside her, scooting away when his knee brushed hers.

"I'm sorry. I never meant to cause any trouble. I flew to the gazebo to hang out for a while."

"Why did you not answer when I called?"

She drew her shoulders toward her ears, shame heating her cheeks. He'd risked his life for her, all because... "Because I wanted to be alone."

Hurt tightened his expression, and his voice came out in a whisper. "I thought he had taken you." His hands rested in his lap, and when she placed hers on top of them, he looked into her eyes.

Crimson cleared her throat. "I'm going to cast a cloaking spell on the house. It will mask the aura of supernatural beings on the property, making the place appear mundane. I'll do a protection spell that will block out anyone with negative intentions too. It'll be bad for business, but I can lift it as soon as this is over."

"Maeve is my number one priority." Gaston sandwiched her hand between his. "All future reservations will be canceled until Olaf's reign of terror has ended."

What had she done? Gaston and his friends had taken her in as if they'd known her forever. They had befriended her, protected her, gone out of their way to make sure she had everything she needed. And in one selfish act, she'd endangered all their lives.

"Thank you, everyone. I didn't think about telling anyone where I was. I'm sorry you went through all that for me."

"What's the point of being immortal if you don't get involved in a little debauchery now and then?" Jane threaded her arm around Ethan's bicep. "But next time, I want to be the one to rack his balls."

"My feisty little nutcracker." Ethan patted her hand. "We'll give you two some space. Call us if you need anything."

"I'll be outside for a few, setting up the spells,

but we'll be out of your hair too." Crimson slipped her hand into Mike's and headed for the door.

Sophie gave her a soft smile before she and Trace headed out, leaving her alone on the sofa with Gaston. She'd had all afternoon and most of the evening to think about everything, and her brain had finally caught up with her heart. Logically, she hadn't known Gaston long enough to feel so strongly about him, but logic rarely mattered where the heart was involved. She knew him in a past life. *Loved* him enough to share her gift with him. She'd be a fool not to give him a chance again.

Plus, the fact he hunted down a murderous monster to save her even though she didn't need saving was sexy as all get-out.

"Maeve..." He laced their fingers together.

"I know about Bridgette," she blurted before he could continue. "I know I was her. And you and I..."

Emotion filled his eyes. Were those tears gathering on his lower lids? He blinked twice, and the moisture disappeared. Now, that would be a nice ability to have. Maeve was one of the unfortunate people who cried when she was angry. Even if she was madder than a gator with his mouth taped shut, tears would stream down her cheeks, making her look weak.

"Why didn't you tell me?" she asked.

"I was afraid I would scare you away. I wanted to help you overcome your aversion to vampires before I hurled an explosive like that."

She nodded, and it was her turn to get misty-eyed. "That was smart."

"Contrary to popular belief, I occasionally make good decisions."

She laughed. "I rarely do."

"Come. Let me show you something." He rose, tugging her up with him. They ascended the stairs and made a right toward the room at the end of the hall. His bedroom.

Her stomach fluttered in anticipation that the thing he wanted to show her was straining behind his zipper. She had fought her attraction to him for long enough.

Sadly, he led her past the bed and opened the closet door. A small cedar box sat on a high shelf, and he pulled it down and handed it to her. "Open it."

She ran her hand across the smooth wood and lifted the lid. Inside lay a lock of red hair the same color as hers, a ticket stub, and an aging photograph lying upside-down. Her throat thickened as she gently lifted the photo from the box. Turning it over, she found her own face staring back at her. "Bridgette," she whispered.

"Yes." His voice was low and husky.

She examined the picture. Bridgette wore a black flapper dress and a brilliant smile. She looked *so* happy. Laying it back in the box, she lifted her gaze to meet Gaston's intense stare. "I wish I remembered this."

He shook his head and returned the box to its place on the shelf. "We aren't meant to remember our past lives. This life, right now, is all that matters, and if you'll allow me, I intend to give you, Maeve O'Meara, every reason to fall in love with me."

"You're doing pretty good so far."

He ran his fingers along her jawline before brushing a thumb over her lips. "Do my fangs still bother you?"

Her heart thumped hard in her chest, his cool, soft touch raising goosebumps on her skin. "Not at all. I think they're sexy."

He smiled, his fangs fully extended. "Good. They are as much a part of me as my exquisite looks and bedroom prowess."

She laughed. "You're awfully sure of yourself."

He stepped closer, lowering his head to whisper in her ear, "Allow me to show you?"

The coolness of his breath made her shiver, and she turned her head toward him, her nose gliding along his cheek, their lips centimeters apart. "Give me your best shot."

He crushed his mouth to hers, the heat in his kiss more than making up for the chill of his skin. With one hand cupping the back of her head, he slid the other down her back and pulled her hips to his.

Oh, my. He was hard all over. Her tongue tangling with his—being careful of his fangs this time—she unbuttoned his shirt and pressed her palms against his toned chest. A growl rumbled beneath her hands, and he shrugged off the garment, dropping it on the floor.

Breaking the kiss, she grinned seductively and tugged her shirt over her head. His gaze wandered down her form before he looked into her eyes. "You are the most beautiful woman I have ever known."

Her cheeks heated. In three hundred years, he'd probably known plenty, so that was quite a compliment. "Would you like to see more of me?" Reaching behind her back, she unhooked her bra and tossed it aside.

"I would like to see *all* of you, *ma chérie*." He

scooped her into his arms and carried her to the bed. "I will worship you like the goddess you are."

He unbuttoned her pants and shoved them to the floor, holding her steady as she stepped out of them and kicked them aside. Thankfully she wasn't wearing shoes, so they came off easily, leaving her in nothing but a pair of black satin panties.

His pupils constricted as he removed his clothes. "Lie down."

She crawled back onto the mattress and lay in the center, her heart thumping like a pair of wings had grown inside her chest. In a flash of speed, he was on her, but he took his time when he got started. His long, slow kiss had her body aching for his touch, and the feel of his hand caressing her side gently yet urgently at the same time had her longing in a way she'd never experienced before.

He slid his hand up to cup her breast and glided his lips down her throat, and devil have mercy, she was overcome with the need to feel his fangs sinking into her flesh.

"I love the way you smell." His breath tickled her skin as he kissed his way down to her chest. "I adore the way you taste." He flicked out his tongue, bathing her nipple before sucking it into his mouth.

Electricity shot from her breast to her core, and

a moan vibrated in her throat. She slid her fingers into his silky hair and closed her eyes, reveling in his form of worship. He continued down, licking, sucking, and caressing every inch of her flesh until he got to her panties.

With a wicked grin, he rose onto his knees, and her gaze locked onto his cock. It was long and thick, and her mouth watered at the sight of it. "Like what you see?" he teased.

"Very much."

He removed her panties and spread her legs, and holy cunnilingus, Batman! Three hundred years of practice had done him good. He slipped a finger inside her while he licked and sucked, rubbing her sweet spot until she cried out in ecstasy. When her breathing finally slowed, he lifted his head and licked his lips. "I'm not finished with you yet."

He better not be. She needed him inside her immediately. Clutching his shoulders, she pulled him to her, taking his mouth in an urgent kiss. She wrapped her hand around his dick, giving two firm strokes before guiding it to her center.

Gaston rose onto his elbows, his ice-blue eyes penetrating her soul. Then his dick penetrated her core. He pressed deep inside her, his gaze never straying from hers as he slid in and out, the delicious friction taking her closer and closer to the edge.

Her entire body hummed, and he looked at her with so much love in his eyes that her chest ached. She ran her hands over his shoulders and down his back. His body was slim yet firm, with definition in all the right places.

"Bite me, Gaston. Drink from me."

He froze mid-thrust. "Are you sure? I do not wish to trigger you in any way."

She grabbed his hips, lifting hers to meet him. "I know it sounds crazy, but I need it. I want to remember...it feels right." Everything about this moment felt like perfection. Familiar, yet brand new at the same time.

With a deep inhale, he lowered himself until their chests met flesh-to-flesh. He nuzzled into her neck, slowly pumping his hips. "You do not have to do this," he whispered. "Being with you is all I need."

"I want you to. Please, Gaston. No glamour. I want to feel it." She gripped his shoulders.

"Very well." He pressed his fangs against her skin and slid his cock out until only the tip remained inside her. With a hard thrust, he bit, and sharp yet pleasurable pain exploded in her neck. He covered the wound with his mouth, moaning as his rhythm increased in intensity.

Sheer ecstasy. It was the only way she could describe it. Every nerve in her body fired on overdrive, and the orgasm that ripped through her shredded her very soul. Gaston cried out, slamming his hips into her one more time, his body shuddering with his release. He swiped his tongue over the punctures and slid his arms behind her back, hugging her tightly.

She lay there, staring at the ceiling, her mind blank as if he had taken every worry, every bad thing that had ever happened to her, and incinerated it. Who knew sex with a vampire could be so life-altering?

No, not just any vampire. She could only feel this way with Gaston. Maybe becoming a vampire herself wasn't such a bad idea.

***

His head spun, a million thoughts racing through his mind, bouncing off each other like a pinball machine. He needed to do something. To tell her how magical the experience had been, but he couldn't make himself move. Making love to

Maeve had been better than he could have ever imagined.

"Gaston? Are you still with me?" She rubbed her hands over his back.

"Yes, *ma chérie*. As I will always be." He lifted his head and smiled drunkenly.

"You got so still it felt like you were dead."

He rolled off her and tugged her to his side. "Apologies. My undead condition can be unnerving for the living. I will try to remember to breathe."

"I don't mind it." She snuggled against him, laying her head on his chest. "Your heart beats so slowly. It's comforting to listen to."

"I'm glad you think so."

She traced her finger along his stomach, making his muscles tighten beneath her touch. "It's not really fair, though."

"What isn't fair?"

She propped her head on her hand to look at him. "That you can remember everything about our past time together, and my first memory of you is a drunk bat biting my hand."

"We will make new memories together. Ones that you can cherish for the rest of your life."

"I like the sound of that."

His eyelids felt heavy, and he could sense the

treacherous sun's ascent. "Dawn is approaching. I will be pulled into the death sleep for a few hours."

"Can I stay and sleep with you?"

"I would love nothing more than to share my bed with you."

FOURTEEN

Two weeks went by with no sign of Olaf. Crimson's cloaking and protection spells were working magically, which, of course they were...she was the most magical witch in all of New Orleans. Maeve stayed at the B and B, spending the days in Gaston's bed and the nights...honestly, they spent a lot of time in bed.

If she stayed inside, she was out of Olaf's reach... as long as no one tipped the bastard off that Bellevue Manor had become her place of refuge. The last of the guests had checked out, and Gaston had canceled the other reservations, so she and he had the entire house to themselves.

She called Addy daily. The sanctuary was running smoothly, with no sign of a predatory vampire lurking in the midst. Everything about the past two weeks had been absolutely perfect. Yet Maeve was stir-crazy, and she could tell Gaston was too. He hadn't hunted at all. His friend Ethan kept them supplied with bottled blood—human for Gaston and cow for Maeve's bat—and Sophie filled his grocery orders.

The Magistrate needed to get his cold, undead ass back to New Orleans so the Council could reconvene and they could end this. She wanted to get back to her bats and to spend time with Gaston without the fear of a death sentence hanging over her head.

"Dinner is served, *ma chérie*," Gaston called from the bottom of the stairs.

Maeve put her phone on the charger and padded down the hall. "You don't have to cook elaborate meals for me every day. At the sanctuary, I survived on ramen and coffee."

"But I enjoy cooking for you." He held out his hand, and she took it as she descended the steps. "It is not often that I get to prepare meals other than breakfast. Perhaps I should change my manor from a bed and breakfast to a dead and dinner."

She laughed. "I think some might take that the wrong way."

"Hmm. I suppose so." He laced his arm around hers and guided her to the dining room. "I hope you like *coq*."

She arched a brow and sank into a chair. "I'd think, after the past two weeks, you would know exactly how I feel about cock."

Heat flared in his icy eyes, and as his lips parted, his fangs extended. A warm shiver ran from the top of her head to the tips of her toes. Gods, how she loved the feel of his fangs on her skin, loved that a simple flirtatious remark could affect him this way.

"You may have to show me again after dinner." He leaned down, taking her mouth in a gentle kiss, and her soul burned.

He pulled away before the flames engulfed them both and gestured to her dinner. A silver serving plate covered in a dome lid sat on the table as it had every night. With a flourish, he removed the cover and set it aside. "*Coq au vin*. As close to my mother's recipe as I can get it."

Her mouth watered at the savory scents of garlic and thyme wafting to her senses. "It smells delicious."

He poured a glass of cabernet for her and a half-wine, half-blood blend for himself. "It's chicken simmered in Burgundy wine with garlic, pearl onions, and mushrooms. Have a taste."

"First, let's toast." She lifted her glass. "I have a homicidal, ancient vampire hunting me and a Council who wants me dead, yet you have made my stay here feel like a vacation in paradise. I feel like a loon, but even with everything going on, I can't think of anywhere I'd rather be than right here, right now."

"Your stay here has been nothing short of paradise for me."

"To making the most out of an unsavory situation. Cheers."

"*Santé.*" He clinked his glass to hers and sipped the contents, watching her over the rim as she drank.

The wine was dry and bold. Perfect for a late-night meal. She sank her fork into her food, the chicken so tender she didn't need a knife. The first bite was a flavor explosion on her tongue. Poultry, wine, onion, garlic...heaven.

"You've outdone yourself, Gaston. You should think about opening a restaurant. Everything you've made for me has been divine."

"You have been a divine inspiration, *ma chérie.* Enjoy."

She took a few more bites, studying his profile as he drank. He had a strong jaw, free of stubble, and cheekbones that would make Spike jealous. He caught her looking, and a sexy smile lifted one corner of his mouth, making her insides flutter. He was smoking hot, kind and generous, a beast in the bedroom, and a perfect gentleman anywhere else. How did she get so lucky?

Okay, aside from the impending doom forcing them to spend all this time together. She may not have remembered anything from their previous lives together, but she was certain of one thing. One absolutely cuckoo thing, or so logic told her.

"What is on your mind?" He angled toward her, his gaze imploring.

She set down her fork and wiped her mouth with a napkin. "Gaston, I..." Her pulse raced, and she rubbed her sweaty palms on her jeans.

He tilted his head slightly, patiently waiting for her to continue. Yet another one of his good qualities. The man had the patience of a kindergarten teacher, but she supposed living for three centuries probably did a number on his concept of time.

His hand lay on the table, and she placed hers on top of his, lacing their fingers together before looking into his eyes. "I'm falling in love with you."

Tears gathered on his lower lids, and he rose to his feet, tugging her up with him. "Ah, *ma chérie*, I have never stopped loving you."

Now her eyes got misty to match his. Her throat tightened around a massive lump, blocking the sob rolling up from her chest. He cupped her face in his hands and brought his lips down to meet hers. She kissed him deeply, wrapping her arms around the back of his neck and holding on like she would never let him go.

"I want to remember," she whispered against his lips. "You loved me then, and you love me now. I want to remember loving you."

He kissed her forehead before holding her with his gaze. "Loving me now is enough."

"No." She shook her head and returned to her chair. "It's not enough. Crimson offered to lead me through a past-life regression, and I want to do it."

He sank next to her, holding her hand on top of the table and gazing at their entwined fingers before he spoke. "Your life was not easy. There are things you will not want to recall. Unnecessary things that aren't worth dredging up."

"You sound like you don't want me to remember."

His eyes tightened. "You were murdered, *ma*

chérie. Stabbed to death in an alley. Surely, you don't want to relive that."

Her stomach soured. No, being murdered was not an event she cared to recall, but she *needed* to remember Gaston. "I'll ask Crimson to pull me out of it before I get that far."

"Maeve..." He tightened his grip on her hand.

"I'm doing it tomorrow. I've already arranged it with her." Kind of. Addy, Sophie, and Crimson planned to stop by the B and B tomorrow before sunset for some girl time. She would text her tonight and ask her if she could perform the spell.

"I know better than to argue when you have that look in your eyes." He released her hand and took a sip from his glass.

"Good. There's something else I wanted to talk to you about." She was on a roll, so she might as well go all in. "I think I want you to turn me."

He coughed mid-sip, and blood dribbled down his chin. Wiping his face with a napkin, he arched a brow. "Why the sudden change of heart?"

"It's not sudden. I've been thinking about it for a while now, and I can't see any drawbacks. I mean, aside from frying in the sun, but I'm already nocturnal. I don't mind drinking blood, I sleep during the day, I'll gain extra powers, and most of all…" She took his face in her hands and kissed his lips.

"Most of all, I'll get to spend forever with you."

His throat bobbed as he swallowed. "As tempting and exquisite as that sounds, I'm afraid I cannot turn you now. It's against the law to turn someone who is under investigation for crimes against a vampire. I would be severely punished."

"Oh." Well, she definitely didn't want him to suffer. "Then, why did you suggest it before? When you first figured out Olaf was after me?"

He sighed. "It was the heat of the moment. I hadn't stopped to consider the consequences."

She clasped her hands in her lap. "Good thing I told you no, then."

"Indeed. Plus, if I turned you now, while you are charged with a crime, you would lose the protection of the red wolf pack. You'd be strictly under vampire law. It's best to wait until your name is cleared."

"Yeah. That's a good point." She couldn't hide the disappointment in her voice, but he was right. Becoming a vampire was a big decision. She needed to spend longer than two weeks thinking about something that would change her very makeup.

"But after." With a finger under her chin, he lifted her gaze to meet his. "There is nothing that would make me happier than to grant you immortality."

"As long as I get to spend forever with you, I'm in."

AFTER DINNER and an exquisite session of lovemaking, Gaston lay in bed beside Maeve, fighting off the death sleep. She already snored softly by his side, the sun having risen an hour ago. His custom-made blinds blocked out the light, but a dim lamp bathed the room in an orange glow.

He had never been happier than at this moment. Maeve loved him, and she wanted to become a vampire and spend eternity with him. His chest swelled with love and gratitude, and he pressed his lips to her forehead.

Her mouth curved upward in a soft smile, and she nuzzled deeper into his embrace.

The past-life regression was a bad idea, but she was adamant about doing it. He could not deny her the experience, not that he held any power over her decisions. But her time in the red-light district wasn't all fun and games. She'd endured far more than any woman ever should.

She moaned softly and stretched her arm across his chest. Whatever she wanted, he would give it to her, and the moment he cleared her name, he would turn her. It killed him to wait when she wanted it now. He'd learned his lesson a century ago, but she needed the protection of the wolves.

"Soon, *ma chérie*. Soon. I will not lose you again." He closed his eyes and was dead to the world.

FIFTEEN

Maeve sat in the living room with Addy, Sophie, Jane, and Crimson. The sun had set half an hour ago, and Ethan had taken Gaston hunting. He'd dug in his heels, wanting to stay with Maeve, but she'd convinced him he needed a guys' night as much as she needed a girls' night. Plus, with Crimson's protection spells on the manor, she was perfectly safe as long as she didn't step outside.

Now she sipped a glass of the chardonnay Sophie brought while Crimson set up some crystals and candles on the coffee table.

"I am so glad I won't be the only vampire chick in our little clique anymore," Jane said. "I get left out of everything."

"We don't try to leave you out, hon." Sophie patted her leg. "We just can't all keep vampire hours."

"That's okay." She flashed a conspiratorial grin. "Maeve and I will be painting the town with blood in no time."

"You bet we will." She couldn't fight her smile. These women had accepted both her and Addy with open wings, and in a couple of weeks, Maeve had gone from only having one friend in the world to having a friend group that rivaled Monica, Rachel, and Phoebe. She'd gotten a second chance to make a life with her soulmate, and now she was about to gain the memories of her previous incarnation with Gaston.

She set her glass on an end table. "How is this going to work?"

Crimson lit a bundle of sage and wafted the smoke toward her. "As soon as I prepare the space, you'll lie on the couch and close your eyes. I'll lead you into a hypnotic state, and then we'll go back in time in your mind." She said a witchy blessing and extinguished the sage.

"Are you sure you want us all here while you do it?" Addy asked. "We could wait outside."

"My stomach is tied in so many knots I feel like

it'll never come undone. Having all of you here is helping me stay grounded."

"Good, because I am dying to know what Gaston was like back then," Jane said.

"He mentioned there might be things I wouldn't want to remember." She swallowed the sour sensation from the back of her throat. "If I get panicky or something, can you pull me out?"

"We'll keep an eye on you," Crimson said. "And you can pull yourself out whenever you want. Just open your eyes, and you'll be back in the present."

"Good. I don't want to experience my death. Just my time with Gaston."

"That's what the personal items are for." Crimson took Gaston's cedar box from the table and handed it to her. "Hold onto this the entire time. It will help take you to the right life and focus your energy on the things you're trying to remember."

She clutched the box in her arms and lay back on the sofa. How much of Gaston's energy resided in this little chest? How many times had he taken it from the shelf to look at the photo inside? She couldn't begin to imagine.

"Close your eyes," Crimson said, "and take a deep breath... Now let it out slowly as I count backward from ten." She counted, and Maeve tried to clear her mind. "Beginning with the soles of your feet, I want you to focus only on your body, relaxing each muscle before moving on to the next."

Crimson led her through the relaxation, all the way to the crown of her head. The nervous tension she'd been carrying around since she woke up this afternoon slowly drained away, and the edges of her mind went fuzzy.

"I'm going to count backward from five. With each number, you will grow less and less aware of your surroundings, your mind drifting to your time with Gaston." She counted, and Maeve slipped deeper and deeper into the trance.

The fuzziness tunneled her vision. She could hear Crimson speaking something that rhymed. A spell, maybe? Her body tingled, and when her vision cleared, Gaston's blue-eyed gaze and fangy smile filled her view, making her pulse sprint and her stomach flip.

He wore a charcoal suit with a vest and pocket watch, and his hair was styled into the same thick, silky waves he wore today.

"Have you found him?" Crimson's voice cut through the dream. Only this wasn't a dream; it was a memory.

"Yes." She smiled as she spoke. "He's here."

"Great. Spend some time there. Explore the vision and focus on how you felt. The more emotion you can remember, the more vivid the memories will be."

Emotion. Her whole reason for doing this was to remember how she felt about Gaston, and man, oh man, was she head over tail. Walking around inside the memory was a bit like watching a home movie. She could fast-forward through parts she didn't care to relive and slow down the ones she wanted to cherish.

She had moved to New Orleans from Ireland as a child in the late 1800s. Her family was poor, and she had to drop out of school to find work. After she turned eighteen, the work she'd found that paid the best was in the red-light district. That was how she met Gaston.

He was a wealthy businessman. She'd identified him as a vampire the moment he stepped into her room. Maeve had been the only supe in the brothel, and Gaston took to her instantly, never feeding from her until she gave him permission.

They started seeing each other outside of work hours, which was against the rules. Maeve would have been fired for dating a client, so Gaston glamoured the madam and all the women there, making them forget he'd ever been a customer. They were free to date, and they fell in love.

He asked her to stop working. He had more than enough money to take care of her, but she'd been stubborn...no surprise there. She'd insisted on working to repay her debts, so he'd gotten her a job as a waitress at one of the restaurants he owned.

She moved in with him, begging him to turn her so she could be with him forever. But her magic had already begun to change him. He wanted to wait until he'd drunk enough of her blood to gain the ability to shift. She'd agreed, thinking it was only fair. If she was to gain his magic, he should gain hers as well.

So they'd waited, but instead of getting closer, Gaston became distant. He worked all night and slept all day, and she grew more and more distraught. A weight of worry sat heavy in her chest, and she couldn't shake the feeling that he was using her. If he truly loved her, wouldn't he make time for her?

How could she have been so stupid? He was a wealthy socialite, and she was a dirt-poor prosti-tute. What made her think a man like him would want to spend forever with a woman like her? He was after her bat, nothing more.

A sob bubbled up from Maeve's chest, and she pried her eyes open. She'd seen enough...*felt* enough. She dragged her hand down her face and sat up, stretching her neck before chugging the rest of her wine, hoping to chase away the sick sensation churning in her gut.

"Well?" Addy asked. All four of her friends stared at her in anticipation. "Was he as romantic then as he is now?"

She laughed dryly. "More so...until he wasn't."

"What do you mean?" Crimson lit the sage again and wafted it in Maeve's direction. Thankfully, the magical herbs helped to ease the acidic sensation crawling through her veins.

"He didn't love her...me. He was using me." She cradled her head in her hands. It didn't make sense. He could already shift, so what could he possibly have to gain from seducing her now? "All he wanted was my bat. He never intended to turn me."

All four mouths dropped open. "That can't be right," Sophie said.

"That doesn't sound like Gaston at all." Crimson extinguished the sage.

Addy moved to the sofa next to Maeve and patted her knee.

"You need to go back under and try again," Jane

said. "I think you went into the wrong timeline. Gaston has done nothing but gush about you since the moment he saw you. Normally he drinks enough rum-tainted blood to rival Jack Sparrow; I've never seen him stay sober this many days in a row."

"What did you see to make you think that?" Crimson asked.

"It's not what I saw. It's what I felt. He—" Before she could elaborate, the rotating door spun, and Gaston and Ethan stepped through.

Gaston smiled and strode into the living room. "How were the memories, *ma chérie*?"

Maeve's jaw clenched, and a spark of anger ignited in her chest. "I see why you didn't want me to do it."

His brow furrowed in concern. "I'm sorry you had to relive the painful moments."

Her hands balled into fists on her lap. "What's your endgame here? What are you trying to gain this time?"

He cocked his head. "I'm not sure I know what you mean."

"You never planned to turn me then, and you don't intend to now." Adrenaline pumped through her veins, and her pulse sprinted. "And I get it. You wanted my bat, and you got it. I can't figure out what you're trying to get from me in this life, though. I've got nothing to give."

"That's not true." He paced around the loveseat and sank onto the couch next to her. "All I want is you."

She shot to her feet and moved across the room, her emotions trampling over her calm like a stampede of wild horses. She'd allowed herself to fall in love. Opened herself up again for the first time since her family died, and look what happened. "I never should have trusted a vampire."

A collective gasp sounded in the room, and Crimson rose to her feet. "We'll give y'all some privacy. C'mon, Addy. I'll drive you home."

"Call me if you need anything," Sophie said as she followed them out the door.

Jane gave Maeve a sympathetic look. "Hear him out. It'll be worth it."

The room emptied, leaving only Maeve and Gaston. She couldn't look at him, so she paced to the upright piano and lightly ran her fingers over the ivories.

"Please." He stood but didn't move toward her. "Tell me what you saw that caused this reaction."

She scoffed and shook her head. "It's not what I

saw; it's what I felt. Distrust, suspicion, dismay. You promised to turn me, but instead, you let me die."

He flinched. "And the memory of that night haunts me to this day."

"Is that what all of this is about? Are you wooing me, trying to be this perfect man for me out of guilt? Because if so, I don't want anything to do with it."

He closed his eyes, going utterly still. Was she being too harsh? Maybe, but after the hell she'd been through, she couldn't bear to be led on because he felt bad about what he did to her in a previous life.

His lids flew open, and he pinned her with an icy gaze. "You have no idea the depths of my guilt."

Well, then. She had her answer, and it hurt more than she cared to admit. Sinking onto the piano bench, she tapped a key, the note ringing out into the silent room.

Gaston lowered to his knees beside her. "For one hundred years, I have lived with the knowledge that if I had been less selfish, I could have saved you. The anguish I've endured for a century would have crumbled most men. Yes, I am trying to make things right with you in this life, but not out of guilt, *ma chérie*. It is out of love. The love I had for you then and the love I feel for you now. It is unconditional, unending, and deeper than the deepest pits of hell."

Damn, he was good with words. He sounded so sincere, yet she couldn't shake the emotions she'd felt in her past life. If he was sincere, then why would she have felt that way? She closed her eyes, grinding her teeth until her jaw ached.

"Fine. If you want to be a theatrical empress, so be it." He stood and clasped his hands behind his back. "You seem to have made your decision, so I will make mine. I will confess to Rene's murder, and you will be free to return to your sanctuary. I would rather have a stake thrust through my heart than be undead another night without you."

Theatrical...? "Are you nuts?"

"I will send my confession via email right now." He turned on his heel and marched out of the room.

Holy hell. She couldn't let him do that. Whether he loved her or not, he didn't need to die for her. "Gaston, wait. Don't do this."

She trailed him into his office and found him squinting at the screen, the blue light on his face enhancing his strong jaw and cheekbones. "Which little picture is the email application? Ethan always assists me where technology is concerned."

"You can't confess to a crime you didn't

commit." She closed the laptop, barely missing his fingers.

"I do not wish to live without you. This will ensure I do not have to." He grabbed her hand, trying to remove it from the computer, but she refused to budge. Of course, with his super-strength, he could have tossed her across the room like a bag of potato chips. Instead, he huffed and crossed his arms.

Who was the drama queen now?

She crossed her arms, mimicking his posture, and studied him, Jane's words echoing in her mind. *Hear him out. It'll be worth it.* Everything about him was worth it...or so she'd thought until she did that stupid past-life regression. This was ridiculous. She needed to give him a chance to explain. Maybe there was a reason she'd felt dismayed. Maybe it had nothing to do with Gaston.

She sucked in a breath to ask him to explain. Instead, she said, "Olaf has to pay for his crimes." Yeah, admitting she might have been wrong was harder than she thought it would be.

His gaze snapped to hers. "You are right. I cannot leave you unprotected while my sire is hunting you. We will first bring Olaf to justice.

Then, I will commit my own crime that is punishable by stake."

She let out a slow breath, the anger draining from her body as she sat in the chair across from him. "Let's back it up a minute, okay? We're both feeling some really strong emotions, and I don't want to do or say anything I'll regret. And I definitely don't want to see you dead."

"I am rather fond of being undead. Maeve..." He leaned forward, folding his arms on the desk. "Please tell me about your regression. Perhaps I can shed light on your unwelcome emotions."

She clasped her hands in her lap and lowered her gaze. "In the beginning, when I first met you, the emotions were very welcome. I loved you so much. But after I moved in with you, you became distant. You were always working, and then you'd sleep all day. And I know that's normal for a vampire, but I also know that you only need a couple of hours of death sleep. I've seen you up well past dawn."

"Oh, my dear Maeve. I..." He ran a hand through his hair. "I was working too much. I'd opened a new restaurant and won a seat on the Council. I let it occupy too much of my time, lost track of what truly mattered. I never knew Bridgette...*you* felt that way."

"Yeah, well, I did. I wanted you to turn me so bad, but you didn't. You didn't really want me...a working girl. You wanted my bat."

In the literal blink of her eye, Gaston left his chair and kneeled in front of her, resting his hands on her legs. "And when you encountered these emotions, that is when you left the memory?"

"It was all I cared to remember."

"I was planning to turn you the night you died. I called the restaurant and spoke to you the moment I was able to shift. I was planning to meet you outside the building, but I was running late. I..." He clutched her hands and lowered his head to press his lips to them

"I am so sorry. Please forgive me." His shoulders rocked with his deep sob.

Well, wasn't this fan-flapping-tastic? She'd accused him of using her, of trying to ease his guilt with her in this life when, if she had only stayed in the regression a little longer, she'd have known the truth.

"Hey." She brushed his hair back, and he lifted his head. Tears stained his cheeks, making her heart wrench. "*I'm* sorry. I should have talked to you about it before I accused you. I don't know what I was thinking."

"You were *feeling*, and if you will give me the chance, I will make sure you never feel that way again."

She held his face in her hands and wiped away his tears. "I love you. That's the only feeling that matters."

***

"AND I LOVE YOU." Gaston rose and tugged her into an embrace. "Please, *ma chérie*. You are the only thing that matters to me in this world. What do I need to do to prove this to you?"

She looked up at him and gave her head a tiny shake. "Nothing. You don't have to do anything else. I should be asking you what I need to do. I'm so sorry I jumped to conclusions."

He pressed his lips to her forehead. "We both behaved somewhat theatrically."

A laugh rolled up from her chest. "Yeah, we did. Still..." She ran a finger down his chest, hooking it into the waistband of his pants. "I'd like to show you how sorry I am."

"Hmm." He gripped her hips. "I suppose a little proof might help ease the sting."

With a wicked grin, she undid his belt and trousers before shoving them to the ground and palming his cock. He hardened instantly, his fangs elongating and his mouth watering with need.

Dropping to her knees, she yanked down his underwear and took his length into her mouth. The warmth and wetness engulfing him made his legs tremble. He rested a hand on the desk to steady himself, but it wasn't enough. He was overcome with emotion, the thought that he'd nearly lost her making his knees buckle.

"Are you okay?" She stood and grasped his shoulders.

"I cannot bear losing you again."

"You won't have to. I promise." She kissed his lips as she undid the buttons on his shirt.

A growl rumbled in his chest. He needed her. To be inside her, to claim her, to be a part of her right now. Moving at vampire speed, he stripped her bare. He pinned her against the bookcase, and she gasped before licking her lips and smiling seductively.

"I love it when you're forceful." She ran her hand down his stomach to grip his dick.

"I belong to you, Maeve. Body, heart, and soul." He grabbed her thigh, lifting it over his hip.

"And I belong to you." She guided him to her center, and he filled her.

Never in his entire existence had he felt more complete. The past hundred years of anguish were well worth the suffering now that he and his dear, sweet Maeve were together again.

Gripping the back of his neck, Maeve lifted her other leg, wrapping them both around his waist. He groaned at the erotic sensation and turned to press her back against the wall. He thrust harder and faster until she cried out in ecstasy. The sound of her voice, of his name on her lips, sent him over the edge as well.

He leaned into her, riding the wave of his orgasm until her pants slowed into normal breaths. Then he carried her upstairs and made love to her again.

CHAPTER

SIXTEEN

Gaston slid on his blazer and turned to face the mirror. Maeve's reflection smiled back at him, and he wrapped his arm around her waist, tugging her to his side. She wore an onyx silk shirt and matching pants with a pair of red high heels that made his fangs extend and his undead heart skip a beat.

"We make a stunning couple." He kissed her temple, and a blush spread across her cheeks. He would miss her warmth and rosy glow, but having her by his side for the rest of his undead life would be worth it.

"Hell yeah, we do. And I can't wait to stop aging. This Council meeting can't come fast enough."

"It won't be long now, *ma chérie*. As soon as

Ethan and Jane arrive, we'll be on our way." He slipped his hand into hers, and they descended the stairs to wait in the living room.

A week had passed since Maeve's past-life regression, and now that they'd gotten all the misunderstandings understood, their time together had been nothing short of bliss. Well, it would have been bliss if not for Olaf looming somewhere in the city, ready to take from Gaston the one thing he loved most.

"Hey." Maeve patted the back of his hand. "Are you okay? My fingers are losing circulation."

He relaxed his grip. "With the Council's help, we will be rid of Olaf once and for all. He will never take anything from either of us again."

"And you and I can finally have our undead ever after."

"Indeed. Please, allow me to present our case. I am familiar with our judge and jury and will be better able to...what is the turn of phrase? Read the room?"

"Yes, that's it. Be my guest. Those guys give me the creeps."

He kissed the back of her hand, and Ethan's aura tickled his senses. "Our friends have arrived."

They met them on the front porch. Jane wore a red sweater and black pants while Ethan donned dark blue. A group of college-age humans passed by on the sidewalk, probably from the vacation rental two blocks over. To their mundane eyes, Gaston and his friends looked like ordinary people going out to dinner at Commander's Palace rather than a group of vampires ready to stand trial in front of the Magistrate.

"Have you watched the news?" Jane asked.

Before he could answer, she continued, "Three bodies were fished out of the Mississippi over the weekend...all of them drained of blood."

"They found another one in the cemetery too," Ethan said. "Olaf has been on a rampage."

Gaston shook his head. "All the more reason for the Council to clear Maeve and take control of the situation. Come, *ma chérie*. It's time you and Genevieve had a proper introduction." Resting his hand on the small of her back, he led her down the porch steps and toward his black Maserati Quattroporte.

"She's beautiful."

He opened the passenger door, and Maeve climbed inside. Jane and Ethan sat in the back seat, and Gaston slid in on the driver's side. The engine roared to life, and Maeve ran her hand along the inside of the door and then the console.

"This is the nicest car I've ever sat in."

"If you're nice to him, he might let you let you drive her," Jane said.

"As long as you don't run over any fae while you're at it." He arched a brow at Jane through the review mirror, and she stuck out her tongue.

Maeve twisted in her seat to look behind the headrest. "You?"

Jane laughed. "He swears I'll never be allowed behind the wheel again, but I'll wear him down eventually."

"Hmm..." Not likely. He backed out of the driveway and headed for the French Quarter. Thankfully, Mardi Gras season was winding down, and traffic wasn't nearly as horrific as it would have been a few weeks ago.

He parked on the curb across the street from the coven house and opened Maeve's door, holding out his hand. Her palm was cold and clammy, and she cleared her throat nervously, biting her lower lip as they approached the front door. Sophie and Trace arrived, meeting them on the porch.

"I want to thank you. All of you." Maeve rested a hand on Gaston's chest. "If this doesn't go the way we hope it goes, I want you all to know how fan-flapping-tabulous you've been to me. Seriously, I couldn't ask for a better group of people to have my back." Her voice caught on the last word.

"You're one of us," Sophie said.

"And we take care of our own," Jane added. "Don't worry. We've got this."

With the evidence Jane had on her phone, he was certain they did. He pressed the buzzer, and Jeffrey opened the door. "Good evening," Gaston said in his most formal voice.

Jeffrey nodded and stepped aside for them to enter. "The Council is ready for you." He led the way down the hall, and Maeve clutched Gaston's arm as he threw open the double doors.

Tension rolled off her in waves, and he could sense the moisture from her palm seeping into his sleeve. Good thing he'd worn black. He stood to Maeve's left while Trace took up position on her right. Sophie joined Jane and Ethan in the chairs along the wall.

In typical Council fashion, all chairs but the Magistrate's were filled when they walked in. Well, Rene's seat was empty, but there was good reason for that. Reason they were about to put to its final rest if things went well.

Elijah looked as horrid as ever, his scraggly hair and paper-thin skin making him appear more zombie than vampire. The man really needed to get out and insert some fun into his life. The double doors closed behind them, and the Magistrate floated in from behind the dais. The vampires bowed their heads as he took his seat, and while Trace and Sophie held their heads high—which was appropriate for the acting leaders of the pack—Maeve followed Gaston's lead and lowered her head in reverence.

"Welcome back, Ms. O'Meara." The Magistrate steepled his fingers and looked down his nose at her. "As I am still jet-lagged from my trip to the homeland, we will get straight to business. You are charged with the murder of Councilman Rene Richard. Have you proof of your innocence?"

"Ye…" Her voice cracked, and she cleared her throat. "Yes, Your Honor, but I think it's best if Gaston explains. He's the one who got the proof."

"Very well. Gaston, I do hope you can convince me. Proceed."

He unwound Maeve's arm from his and stepped forward. "Have you heard the news of the bodies turning up drained of blood? I believe the humans have found five since Rene's demise."

The Magistrate inclined his head. "I am aware. Finding the culprit is next on our agenda."

"The man who murdered the humans and the man who killed Rene are one and the same."

The Magistrate made a circular motion with his hand, indicating Gaston should get to the point.

His abdomen tightened over his roiling gut as a thought he hadn't considered took hold of his mind. Olaf was Gaston's sire. He was drawn to New Orleans in search of Maeve. If not for them, the murderous vampire wouldn't even be in this city.

Satan's balls. They were to blame, after all...in a way.

His hands curled into fists. He could talk his way out of taking the fall for this, but what about Maeve? It wasn't like she had summoned him, but he knew of one councilman who would blame her, nonetheless. "The killer's name is Olaf, and he is at least five hundred years dead."

"That would explain how he was able to attack a councilman with such ease. How do you know him?"

Gaston's throat turned to a wad of cotton. They couldn't know of Maeve's involvement. If only he had turned her before this trial. At least then, he could have sent her his thoughts and warned her not to reveal her connection. The Council had to believe it was a coincidence. Devil have mercy. If he lost her because he didn't turn her soon enough again, he would shove the stake through his heart himself.

"I'm afraid Olaf is my sire." He stilled, trying his best to listen as the councilmen muttered to each other, but they were masters, as was he. They didn't need to use telepathy to hide their voices.

"Why did you summon him?" the Magistrate asked.

"I didn't. His presence here is nothing more than a coincidence, but he did confess to Rene's murder. Jane has it on video."

"Preposterous!" Eli shot to his feet, and Gaston fought his eye roll. What was it with this fucking guy? His rod must have been smaller than a mini-golf pencil for him to constantly jockey like this. "Vampires of that age do not travel unless they have reason to. They've perfected their hunting and are extremely territorial."

Gaston's nostrils flared. "You lecture me as though I am not 'of that age.' Olaf is not like most vampires. He is a psychopath."

"And you led him into our midst," Eli growled. "For that, you will be punished."

"No!" Maeve stepped forward, and Gaston shot her a look that should have frozen her.

She ignored his warning. "Olaf came here looking for me. He's the one who murdered my colony. He's here to finish the job."

No, ma chérie. Gaston's heart plopped into his stomach to swim with the bitter acid.

The Magistrate leaned forward. "Are you saying you are responsible for this Olaf's presence in New Orleans?"

"No, she is not," Gaston answered.

"Yes, I am. You can't punish Gaston for it. All he's done is help me. Look at the video. You'll see Olaf is the one causing all this mayhem."

The Magistrate regarded her, then cut his gaze to Gaston before looking at Jane. "I will examine the video now."

"You got it." Jane typed on her phone screen. "Turn up the sound."

The Magistrate pulled his phone from within his robes, and the councilmen gathered around him to watch. "This certainly does indicate Olaf as the culprit. Thank you, Jane. Gentlemen, return to your seats."

The men did as they were told, and the Magistrate rose to his feet. "Maeve O'Meara, in the matter of Rene Richard's murder, you have been found innocent."

With her long exhale, Maeve's posture slumped in relief, but Gaston eyed the Council warily, and for good reason. Eli glared at her, his eyes calculating, most likely filling their leader's mind with his horrid thoughts.

The Magistrate nodded. "In the matter of bringing a murderer into our midst, you have been found guilty."

Maeve gasped. "What?"

"The hell she has." Trace stepped forward. "You are forgetting you're dealing with shifters, Magistrate. Innocent until proven guilty."

The Magistrate narrowed his eyes in warning. "You have been *charged*."

"You can't hold her responsible for something she had no idea was happening." Jane strode to the center of the room. "Nobody even knew who Olaf was until Gaston figured it out."

"Someone must be held responsible." *Fucking Eli.*

Gaston stood in front of Maeve. "You lay a finger on her, and I will shove a stake so far up your ass it pierces your heart."

Eli seethed. If it were possible for flames to shoot out his ears, he'd have set the house on fire.

Gaston widened his stance and crossed his arms. No way in all of Satan's realm would he let Maeve take the blame. "If you want to punish her, you'll have to get through me."

"Gladly." Eli shot to his feet once more and pounced.

He latched onto Gaston's shoulders and threw him against the wall with a *thwack*. Stunned for only a brief second, Gaston slid to the ground and landed on his feet. That would be the last hit Eli got on him.

The junior vampire sneered, and Gaston hissed, baring his fangs. *"Protect her,"* he said to Jane and Ethan, and his friends pulled Maeve aside. Sophie and Trace joined to make a protective cage around her.

Gaston plowed into Eli, tackling him. They rolled over each other, Gaston clutching the front of his robes and mustering his willpower not to rip off the councilman's head in the chambers.

"Enough!" The Magistrate boomed, and Gaston released his hold before rising to his feet. "No punishment has been determined, Elijah. Mind yourself."

Eli scrambled to his feet and spat at Gaston's

shoes. "She's nothing but a shifter. They come in here thinking they can tell vampires what to do. Our kind is far superior to these mongrels, and it's time we started acting that way."

He shot toward Gaston's friends, and before they realized what was happening, he sank his fangs into Trace's neck. The wolf shifter screamed. The Magistrate lifted a hand, and Eli froze. Gaston took his arm and pried the unruly imbecile off the wolf pack's acting leader.

In a flash of magic and falling clothes, all three shifters called on their animals. Maeve swooped upward and circled the vampires while Trace and Sophie crouched low, preparing to attack.

"Alfred," the Magistrate called in his henchman. "Take Eli to a holding cell. He is guilty of biting a shifter. If a war begins, he'll be found guilty of that too."

Alf slapped a pair of enchanted shackles on Eli and dragged him out of the room. The Magistrate straightened his robes, and Gaston cast his gaze to the ceiling, where Maeve roosted on a chandelier. He wanted to tell her she was safe to come down, but he wasn't sure how the Magistrate planned to proceed. So, he gave her the most comforting look he could pull off at the moment, and she stayed put.

The Magistrate tucked his arms into his sleeves and addressed the shifters. "Please accept my humblest and most sincere apologies for the behavior of my councilman. He will be punished to the fullest extent, and I do hope our truce can remain intact. Elijah's views do not represent those of the coven."

Trace looked at Sophie before glancing at Gaston and then at his discarded clothes.

"I believe they would like a moment to dress before negotiations begin," Gaston said.

"Very well. Follow me." The Magistrate scooped up their clothes and started for the door that led to the offices. Sophie and Trace followed, and Maeve flew down to land on Gaston's shoulder.

"Come, *ma chérie*. I will not let anyone harm you." He took Maeve into a private office and waited for her to dress.

"Am I off the hook?" Concern filled her sea-green eyes, making his heart ache.

"I'm not sure." He wrapped his arm around her shoulders. "Now would be a time when the mind-reading abilities you thought I had would come in handy. The Magistrate can be a hard nutshell to open."

They returned to the Council's chamber, and

Ethan and Jane flanked them. *"Let us know what you need,"* Ethan said.

"We'll fight to the death if we have to," Jane said, and Gaston's chest swelled with gratitude. He had the most wonderful friends.

Trace and Sophie returned to the room, and she joined Gaston while Trace faced the Magistrate. "According to the truce established more than a century ago, an attack on any shifter is grounds for war. An attack on the acting alpha is a clear declaration."

The Magistrate nodded once. "I understand."

"But..." Trace held up a finger. "I am willing to maintain the truce under two conditions."

"Name them," the Magistrate said.

"Eli will never hold office in your coven again."

"Done." He snapped his fingers at the remaining council members, and they nodded their agreement. "He will be staked tonight. What is your second condition?"

Trace glanced at Maeve and winked. "That Miss O'Meara be cleared of any and all charges. She can resume her normal life with no debt owed to the vampires."

Something akin to both a sob and a laugh burst

from Gaston's throat. He had the most wonderful friends, indeed.

"Your generosity is greatly appreciated." The Magistrate bowed. "I agree to your terms."

"Yes!" Maeve jumped and threw her arms around Gaston's neck. He lifted her, spinning in a circle before resting her feet on the floor.

"Trace." Keeping one arm wrapped around his love, Gaston shook the shifter's hand. "I cannot thank you enough."

"It's what friends are for."

"There is still the matter of ridding our city of your sire," The Magistrate said. "Gaston, the entire coven is at your disposal. Let us know how you would like to proceed. We will reconvene tomorrow night and plan our attack."

"Great," Sophie said. "Now, let's get out of here before they decide to charge us with anything else."

Gaston bowed at the Magistrate and led his friends out the door. While he would have enjoyed watching Eli get the stake, turning Maeve was his first concern.

When they reached the sidewalk, Jane patted his shoulder. "I'm sure you two have some cele-brating to do before she becomes a creature of the night, so we'll catch a ride home with Sophie."

"I appreciate that." He smiled at Maeve, and she returned the gesture with a sparkle in her eyes.

His friends turned the corner, and Maeve stepped off the sidewalk, heading to Genevieve. He started to follow, but a disturbance in the air gave him pause. His skin pricked, and icy panic rushed through his veins.

"Mae—" Before he could finish speaking her name, she disappeared.

Olaf had taken her.

SEVENTEEN

He literally came from nowhere. Okay, everybody came from *some*where, but all Maeve knew was that one minute she was walking with Gaston toward his car and a nanosecond later, Olaf the Destroyer had tossed her over his shoulder in a fireman carry and booked it out of town.

She'd witnessed Gaston's vampire speed. He could go from one end of the house to the other in no time flat. Even Jane, who was supposedly only a few years dead, had zipped in and out of the house in a blur right in front of her. But this guy...

Imagine Usain Bolt as a vampire. Now quadruple his speed. Yeah, that fast.

Brisk March air cut through her silk shirt,

stinging her skin. Streetlights smeared into solid streaks, and her vision began to tunnel. Whether it was from shock or going warp speed, she didn't know, but she could not let herself pass out in this psychopath's presence.

His rock-hard shoulder dug into her gut, and she used her position to her advantage. Wrapping her arms around his waist, she opened her mouth and chomped down on his lower back. Sadly, her blunt human teeth couldn't tear into his flesh like a set of fangs would, but much to her satisfaction, the vampire yelped.

Then he stopped...undead in his tracks...and released his hold. Maeve flew backward...or foreword—her brain was so scrambled she couldn't tell which way was up—and the back of her head smacked the concrete. A cracking sound exploded in her ears, and she barely had time to hope it was the road and not her head before her tunneling vision turned to pinpricks.

So much for not passing out in his presence. Darkness engulfed her.

When she came to, she lay on the cold Formica counter. Her head throbbed, and her vision wavered on the overhead light no one had bothered to turn on. Was she in the sanctuary?

She groaned and rolled to her side, spilling the gourmet breakfast Gaston had made for her all over the tile floor. With her stomach empty, she pushed to sitting and nearly vomited again. Addy lay on the floor, blood oozing from her temple, Olaf curling his lip at her in disgust.

"What a waste of shifter magic." He turned his menacing gaze on hers, his blue pupils so pale they were almost nonexistent. "Who in their right mind would want to transform into vermin?"

"Addy." She tried to stand, but before the command made it from her brain to her muscles, Olaf pinned her to the table, his fingers wrapped around her throat.

"You'll stay where I put you, little girl. I won't have you getting away again." He smiled, and spit dripped from one fang like a drooling bloodhound. "Your friend is alive for now. I had planned to kill you and turn her as my witness, but I despise rats. Plague-carrying parasites."

Oh, boy. This was not good. Not good at all. *There's the understatement of the century, Maeve.* She thought back over all the serial killer documentaries and crime shows she'd binged on her nights off. The women who got away were always smart. They played on the killer's ego. She had to keep him talking about himself. Murderers loved to monologue.

"How did you find me?" she squeaked, and he loosened his grip on her throat.

"You didn't make it easy, hiding out in this devil-forsaken place. I searched your surname for years, but you weren't registered anywhere...until you inherited this." He gestured to the room like it disgusted him. "I had been watching you for days. Then I saw Gaston, one of my witnesses, leaving your place of business, and I was intrigued."

"What about Gaston could intrigue a mighty vampire like you?" She cleared her throat, and he finally released his grip. She didn't dare try getting up, though. "You're the most extraordinary vamp I've ever seen." *That's it. Stroke that ego.*

His lips twitched into an almost smile. "That is true."

She took a moment to study his face, forcing as much awe into her expression as she could. With his fair skin, impressive height, and blond hair that was shaved on the sides and braided down the middle, he looked like he belonged in the battle of Ragnarök. Hell, maybe he really was there. Everything about him screamed Viking.

Addy stirred, rising onto her elbow and rubbing

her bloody temple. She looked at Maeve, her eyes widening in alarm, and pushed to sitting. Olaf stroked his chin with his thumb and forefinger, still enjoying Maeve's faux admiration, but Addy's movement drew his attention. He started to turn his head, so Maeve gritted her teeth and touched the bastard. She placed her hand on his stubbly cheek and turned his face toward hers.

Keep him talking. "How many animals can you turn into now?"

"Only five, though there is a congregation of gator shifters I plan to visit when I'm done with you."

Addy shifted and skittered out of the room. Why hadn't Maeve done the same? Shock. She would blame this entire ordeal on shock and Olaf's faster-than-the-flash super speed. She had escaped him once in bat form. She could do it again, couldn't she? Anything was better than lying here and becoming his next meal.

"Gators, huh? That'll be *so* cool." She called on her bat and shifted, shooting upward and flying toward the open door.

Olaf let out a maniacal laugh. "Oh, you naughty girl. I've made my decision. You will both die."

He turned into a bat and flew after her. Based on

his speed in vamp form, he was surprisingly slow in the air. Maeve flapped with all her might, heading straight for the hoary bats' hunting grounds. Her charges had become territorial. It took weeks to introduce a new bat into the colony, and she was counting on their instinct to protect their land to kick in with Olaf, the intruder, in their midst.

The hoaries squeaked, welcoming her home, but as Olaf approached, they attacked. Five bats flew toward him, circling and diving in, knocking him around like a pinata. Sadly, his guts didn't spill out like candy. Instead, he shot toward her, a shifter-seeking missile. He'd been toying with her before. His super speed transferred into his bat, after all.

She flew toward the roost, but her bat was no match for his. He shifted mid-air, grabbed her around her belly, and drifted to the ground as lightly as an angel feather. Maeve squealed, and a buck-naked Addy barreled toward him, wielding a stake from the office arsenal and screaming like a warrior princess.

"Enough," Olaf shouted, and he swung his arm, knocking Addy upside the head and sending her careening into the roost wall. She crumpled to the ground, unmoving. Again. How many times could a shifter be knocked unconscious before it affected her brain? Hopefully it was more than two.

Maeve struggled against Olaf's grip. She twisted, shimmying her little bat shoulders, hoping she could wiggle out of his clutches, but she was small and his hand engulfed her entire body from butt to neck. So, she did what any respectable bat would do in a situation like this. She leaned her furry face down and bit him.

His flesh was tough, nothing like the papery-skinned Elijah from the Council, and definitely not like Gaston's soft, smooth skin. Olaf could really use an industrial-strength moisturizer.

Even still, her fangs pierced his thumb. If he were human, blood would have gushed from the wound, but as she pulled her mouth away, only the two small punctures marred his skin, and they were already beginning to heal.

Olaf glowered at her and marched toward the building where the bats roosted. He flung open the door and slammed it behind him, hurling Maeve to the dirty floor. Yeah, bats pooped where they roosted. The floor was covered in guano, and now she was too. *Fan-flapping-tastic.*

Oh well. She'd worry about cleaning the crap

from her fur later. Right now, she needed to fly like a bat out of hell.

But there was a problem with her plan. She tried to flap her wings, but she couldn't move. An invisible force pinned her to the ground. She lay on her back with her wings spread wide as if she were an offering to an ancient god. There was nothing godly about the vampire who stalked toward her, his lips peeled back in a sneer.

The skin around his eyes tightened like he was concentrating. Or maybe he was constipated; it was hard to tell. Her body tingled, her magic coming to life against her will. *No way.* He drew her human form to the surface, forcing her to shift right there on the ground. Yeah, she was naked too. She tried to move her arms, to cover her girly bits, but the bastard had her pinned spread eagle.

She ground her teeth, fighting against his glamour to no avail. Despite the chilly March air, sweat beaded on her forehead. "Don't you have better things to do than pick on a little bat? Or do you always hunt people who are weaker than you?"

He smirked, dropping to his knees beside her. "Everyone is weaker than me."

Her heart thrummed, her breath coming in short pants. She wanted to punch him. To claw his eyeballs out and feed them to him. But his glamour was too strong. She was paralyzed everywhere except her mouth, so she cleared her throat and hocked up the biggest wad of saliva and phlegm she could. Then she spit in his face.

Mucus dripped down his cheek, and he flicked it away with a finger. With a palm against her forehead, he turned her head, angling it until her neck muscles screamed with the tension. His fangs pierced her skin, tearing her flesh open, which was totally unnecessary. Gaston only made two small punctures when he drank from her. Then again, Olaf wasn't just looking for a snack. He planned to drain her.

The nasty piece of work went to town, making slurping noises as he drank. You'd think that with five hundred years of experience, his feeding skills would have been more refined, but no. He sounded like a three-year-old glugging down a sippy cup of chocolate milk.

"Gaston is going to tear you apart," she ground out.

Olaf lifted his head, and blood was smeared across his face like that same three-year-old had gotten ahold of a birthday cake. "I welcome him to try." He bent over and continued his meal.

Welp, this is it, Maeve. We've had a nice run. At least she wouldn't have to live in fear anymore. And Gaston... He and the rest of the New Orleans coven would track this bastard down and end his cursed existence for good. She had no doubt of that. No more families would die from Olaf stealing their magic.

Coldness seeped into her bones. Her head spun, and her entire body felt light, as if she were floating. As her vision blurred, her heart slowed, and the throbbing in her temples became unbearable.

Then it stopped, and blissful darkness engulfed her.

EIGHTEEN

Gaston floored Genevieve, zipping around traffic and pushing his car to her max. Two hundred miles per hour wasn't nearly fast enough with his precious Maeve's life on the line. He came to a screeching halt in front of the sanctuary and rushed to the door, but it was locked. No noise emanated from inside.

Resting his hand on the wall to steady himself, he called on his magic, searching the vibrations in the atmosphere for Olaf. The second his sire registered in his senses, he took off, practically flying through the grass as he made his way around the back of the main building.

A naked woman lay motionless in the grass, and Gaston froze, his heart leaping into his throat and lodging there. No, he couldn't be too late. He *refused* to be too late.

He moved toward her, and relief pulled his heart back into his chest where it belonged. "Adelaide?"

She opened her eyes and rubbed her forehead. "Gaston?"

"What happened?"

"Olaf. He has Maeve." She pointed to the outbuilding as she scrambled to her feet. "You have to help her. I'll go call for backup."

He nodded and sent a message to Ethan in his mind, *"Meet me at the bat sanctuary. He has Maeve."*

Addy shifted and scurried away, and Gaston threw the door open to find his sire bent over a woman covered in blood. Maeve. She lay on the ground, her neck ripped open, her chest not moving to indicate she could take a breath.

They call it blind rage for a reason. Gaston's vision tunneled until all he could see was a ring of fiery red and his target. Without warning, without a hiss, without so much as a "Stop that, you fiend!" Gaston barreled toward Olaf, plowing into the ancient vampire and ripping him away from poor, defenseless Maeve.

She made a pained gurgling sound when Olaf

released his magical hold, and Gaston's heart wrenched in his chest.

"What have you done to her?" he snarled, throwing his sire onto his back and straddling him, pinning his shoulders with his hands.

Olaf licked his lips and smiled. Dark red blood stained his teeth and tongue. "What I should have done years ago. To her. To you. To every witness I spared. None of you have ever shown appreciation for the gift I gave you."

Gaston backhanded him across the face, splitting the bastard's lip on a fang. "How could we after everything you took?"

"Your families would have died eventually. I gave you eternal life."

Gaston landed a punch square on his jaw, knocking it from its socket. "I never asked for it."

Olaf stretched his mouth, popping the dislocation back into place. "Time to end this, you ungrateful piece of swamp slime." He flung his arms, knocking Gaston to the ground. With speed faster than lubed-up lightning, he shot to his feet and planted a boot in Gaston's stomach.

The air he had drawn in to curse his sire came out in a whoosh, nearly taking his lungs with it. Tears blurred his eyes, and as he curled onto his side, he watched Maeve's fingers twitch. She was still alive, and that was all the motivation he needed to drag his ass up and fight this fiend to the death.

Olaf made a *tsk* sound through his teeth. "I am two hundred years older than you, boy. You don't stand a chance."

"My power may pale in comparison to yours, but I have something you will never have. The love of a woman and a group of friends to give me strength you could never imagine." He bared his fangs and hissed.

Olaf hissed in return, and they ran for each other. Gaston reached for his throat, but his sire easily sidestepped him, swinging an arm into Gaston's back. With his own momentum and Olaf's extra push, he careened into the wall, busting through the wood and landing fangs first in the grass outside.

His pride was the only thing bruised in that maneuver, though. He jumped to his feet and ran back for more, this time landing another punch before Olaf threw him through the wall again.

"Keep this up, and we'll tear the building down." Olaf laughed and made a *bring it* motion with his fingers. "Is this all you've got, young one?"

Gaston roared and charged. Olaf rolled his eyes

and threw him against the wall yet again. A rusty machete hung on the opposite wall, but as Gaston lunged for it, Olaf tripped him. He rolled through the bat poop, landing on his hands and knees.

"This fight has grown tiresome." He picked Gaston up by the throat and slammed him into the ground. Gaston clawed at his hands and kicked his legs, trying desperately to regain control, but his strength was no match for his sire's.

Olaf tilted his head, studying him with an amused expression on his blood-stained face while pressing harder and harder against Gaston's throat. If he had needed to breathe, he would have suffocated, but blocking his airway wasn't Olaf's intention. His claws dug into Gaston's skin, his grip growing tighter than a vise as he began twisting. He planned to tear Gaston's head off.

Death by decapitation was not the way Gaston wanted to go. Especially not here, in front of a dying Maeve. He turned his head ever so slightly to see her. She stared back, her mouth agape, the light fading from her eyes.

Then a look. Recognition dawned in her gaze, and she stretched her fingers toward him. "Gaston, kill him," she managed to whisper before her lids fluttered shut.

Maeve's words filled him with a strength he'd never known before. *Anything for you, ma chérie.* A guttural growl rumbled in his chest. It would have come out as a primordial scream if his throat wasn't currently smashed like a kinked garden hose. Instead, it fueled him, anger burning white hot in his chest.

He boxed Olaf's ears and then grabbed them, using them as handles to slam him onto his side. With renewed strength and speed, he shot toward the machete, yanking it from the wall and spinning, his arm outstretched, toward Olaf's advance.

In the stories he would tell of this in the future, the machete will have taken his sire's head clean off. In reality, the dull, rusty blade merely severed the neck halfway through. Gaston had to hack him four more times before grabbing a handful of blond braid and finally tearing his head from his shoulders. Messy, yes, but quite effective.

The old vampire's body twitched once and then turned into a pile of ash.

"Maeve. *Ma chérie,* I am here." He dropped to his knees beside her and rested a hand on her chest. She wasn't breathing. He cradled her face with his palm. Her skin was deathly cold, her complexion sickly white.

He bit his wrist, tearing his flesh and massaging his arm to force his sluggishly thick blood to flow. As a bead of red formed on his skin, he pressed the wound to her mouth. "Drink, my love. Please. I cannot lose you again."

He rubbed his arm, moving the blood from his elbow to his wrist, filling her mouth with his essence. Olaf had drained her to the point of death. If Gaston were to be successful in turning her, he would have to drink from her too. He couldn't bear to suck from the gash his sire had torn, so he gently pierced her shoulder with his fangs. He sucked, but nothing came out of the wound.

"No, my dear, sweet Maeve. You must have something left for me." He bit again, deeper this time, and covered the punctures with his lips, sealing them around it and sucking for all he was worth. Finally, a drop. Then another. He sucked one more time, and a tiny trickle bathed his tongue. That would have to be enough.

He activated his glamour, focusing his magic into her. She swallowed, and her lids flew open. "There you are," he said as he pressed his wrist against her lips. "Drink. Take all you need."

As she sucked his wrist, he focused on forming a tether between them. Not only the connection of a sire with his offspring, but the unbreakable bond of a vampire and the woman he loved. His mating mark shined bright in her aura. When she awoke undead, he would teach her how to mark him, binding them together for eternity.

She drank deeply. Too deeply, if he were being honest, but she needed the blood more than he did. He could feel his strength waning, his eyelids growing heavy. He would need to refuel soon.

With a gasp, she sat bolt upright. Her neck wound began to heal, and she turned her head toward him. Her lips curved into a sweet smile, and love filled her eyes. "You came for me."

"I will never leave you alone." His head spun, and nausea churned in his stomach. So, this was what it felt like to bleed out.

She rested her palm against his cheek. "Olaf?"

He gestured to the pile of ash. "He'll never bother you again."

"I love you, Gaston."

"And I love you, *ma chérie*. Forever."

Her eyes widened like giant doughnuts, and she flopped onto her back. The death sleep had pulled her under. Gaston tried to stand, but his knees buckled. He'd given her too much.

"Ethan, I need blood," he called one last time

before taking off his shirt and stretching it across Maeve to cover her torso. He couldn't keep his eyes open, so he lay beside her, resting his hand on her stomach.

"Found him," Ethan's voice floated into the room, and Gaston opened his eyes into slits. Addy and Jane joined him in the building.

Jane kicked her foot through the ash. "Is this Olaf?"

"Yes," Gaston whispered.

"Good riddance. C'mon. Let's get you two home before the sun rises."

"Blood?" Gaston asked. If he didn't get some into him soon, he wouldn't be recovered by the time Maeve awoke. He *had* to be there for her.

Ethan grabbed his arm, tugging him to his feet and slinging it over his shoulders to support his weight. "You've got a fridge full at home."

"I brought Maeve a blanket and some more of her clothes." Addy offered them to Ethan, who tucked them under his free arm. "Take good care of her."

"Always," Gaston muttered.

"I've got Maeve." Jane took the blanket and draped it over her before cradling her in her arms. Maeve's head lolled back, but thankfully her neck wound had completely healed. She would be good as new tomorrow night.

Ethan helped Gaston into the back seat of Genevieve, and Jane laid Maeve across his lap.

"Ethan, do you want to take our car, and I'll drive Genevieve?" Jane asked.

Gaston gave her a hard glare, and she laughed. "I'm kidding. I'll see y'all at the manor."

Ethan slid into the driver's seat and started the engine. "Good goat cheese, y'all stink."

Gaston leaned his head back and closed his eyes. "Such can be expected when you roll around in batshit."

Ethan chuckled and pulled the car onto the road, heading for Gaston's...and now Maeve's... home. When they arrived, Jane carried Maeve to the bath while Ethan took Gaston to the kitchen to refuel.

He didn't bother heating his meal. He chugged an entire carafe of O Positive, gulping it down like it was the best thing he'd ever tasted. His head stopped spinning, but he would need the death sleep to restore him fully.

He quickly showered, and when he arrived in his bedroom, he found Maeve nestled in the sheets. Jane had cleaned her up and dressed her in a black satin nightgown, befitting the queen of the night she was about to become.

"Thank you for your assistance," he said to Jane and Ethan, who stood in the doorway. "You are good friends."

"Any time, old man." Jane winked and then wrapped her arm around Ethan's waist. "C'mon, babe. Let's leave the lovebats to their death sleep."

Gaston nuzzled next to Maeve, draping his arm across her shoulders and resting his head on the pillow next to hers. He could have lain there all day watching the transformation take hold, her complexion turning to porcelain, her hair shiny and lusher than ever. But it wasn't long before the death sleep claimed him too.

CHAPTER

NINETEEN

"You make such a beautiful vampire bride." Addy pinned a tiny black rose in Maeve's hair and smiled at their reflections in the antique vanity mirror.

Maeve smiled back and gasped at her fully extended fangs. It had been two months since Gaston turned her, but she didn't quite have control of her vampireyness yet. He assured her she would in time, and she trusted him with all of her being.

She wore a black ball gown for the wedding. Hey, if she was going to be a vampire, she was going all in. Her nails were silver, and she'd painted her lips dark red. Addy's maid of honor gown was pewter in color to match Ethan's suit. The rest of her newfound friends waited in the garden outside.

Gaston had marked her as his mate when he turned her, and a week after she awoke, she gained enough magic to mark him too. They were bound for eternity, and a wedding wasn't necessary. But she'd be damned if she'd give up her dream of a heartfelt ceremony and fancy party. Gaston seemed delighted to plan it with her, and they had turned his mansion into a party venue to rival the Met Gala.

"Are you ready?" Addy asked.

"I've never been more ready for anything in my life." She rose from her perch on a stool, and Addy fluffed out her dress. They made their way down the stairs, and she paused to take in the reception area. The ballroom held tables draped in black linen with silver candles and black roses as centerpieces.

Gaston had moved all the furniture out of the living area, making room for a buffet and bar. They had black teacups with little bats painted on the inside and pewter goblets for the wine and blood. Everything was perfect, especially the man she was about to marry.

They walked to the back door, and if Maeve were still a simple shifter, her heart would have been beating out of her chest. Instead, the sluggish muscle beat hard against her ribs once. Five seconds later, it beat again. Apparently, this was the vampire equivalent of a racing pulse.

Addy walked out the back door first and made her way down the aisle. Maeve peeked out the window and smiled. She hadn't seen Gaston yet today, and the branches of the magnolia tree blocked him from her view. The first time she saw her soon-to-be husband would be when it was her turn to walk down the aisle.

Her throat thickened, and pressure built behind her eyes. The emotions swirling in her soul made her want to race out the door, shout *I do*, and throw herself into Gaston's arms. But she was a big girl; she could control herself. She hoped.

Addy took her place near the alter, and all the guests stood, waiting for Maeve's entrance. The front row held Jane, Sophie and Trace, and Crimson and Mike. Katrina and Gabe stood behind them with Asher and Jasmine, who looked none too comfortable in the presence of so many vampires, but it was nice of her to show. Destiny, the angel who baked their four-tiered cake—red velvet with magical black frosting that she promised wouldn't stain anyone's teeth—stood next to Jasmine.

Maeve swallowed the thickness from her throat, took a deep—and totally unnecessary—breath, and strode out the door. She reached the bottom of the porch steps, and Gaston came into view. He stood at the end of the aisle with Ethan on one side, the Magistrate on the other. His black suit fit him perfectly, accenting his lean build. His dark hair flowed in thick waves, and devotion filled his ice-blue eyes.

Her chest tightened. Never did she ever think she would be capable of loving anyone...much less a vampire...this much. Her lips curved into a smile, showing off her extended fangs, and she walked toward the most perfect man ever created. Her soulmate.

GASTON ACHED at the sight of her. The black gown she chose made her porcelain skin glow ethereally in the moonlight, and her fiery red hair and sea-green eyes called to him like the most beautiful symphony ever written. She was lovely. Everything he never dared dream he could have.

She was his mate, and now, she would be his wife.

She reached the altar, and he took her hand, bringing it to his lips to kiss her fingers. Her smile brightened her eyes, and her fangs... Every time he saw them extended, he got a hell of a hard-on. Now was no exception. Good thing he'd opted for briefs beneath his trousers. They kept the beast contained.

Keeping her hand clasped in his, they turned to face the Magistrate.

"We are gathered beneath the cloak of night to join Gaston Bellevue and Maeve O'Meara in unholy matrimony. If anyone has a reason for this union not to happen, speak now or forever hold your tongue."

A pop sounded from behind them, followed by a flash of heat. "Oh, damn. Sorry I'm late."

Gaston turned, his brow shooting toward his hairline as he took in the uninvited guest. He wore a dark red suit with an even darker tie, and his black hair was slicked to his head in a classic TV villain style.

"Who is that?" Maeve whispered.

"Satan," Gaston said, feigning delight. "To what do we owe the honor?"

"I heard there was going to be a party, and I didn't want to miss it. Proceed." He waved flippantly and took a seat in the back row.

Gaston couldn't very well tell the king of Hell to

leave, so he turned to face the Magistrate once more. "Let's continue."

The Magistrate nodded. "Face each other and say your vows, please."

Gaston took both Maeve's hands in his and gazed into her eyes. "Maeve, *ma chérie*, you have no idea how happy you have made me. Despite the wonderful friendships I have made over the years, I was a lonely, miserable wretch."

Ethan chuckled, and Gaston cut him a look. Yes, he may have used those same words to describe his best friend at some point, but it was true. They were quite the pair.

"Maeve," he continued, "I promise to love you with every fiber of my being for the rest of my death. I will cherish you, worship you, and make sure that your every need is met for eternity. Even if we cross into Satan's realm, I will find you and do whatever it takes to be by your side."

Pressure built in the back of his eyes, and a tear slid down his cheek. "I love you so much. You are everything." He slid a platinum band onto her finger.

She blinked rapidly and swallowed hard. "Wow. How do I follow that?"

The audience chuckled, and she wiped a tear

from her cheek. "Gaston, I think I do have an idea of how happy I make you because you make me the happiest woman alive... I mean undead. I've lost so much in my life, and now, in my death, I have gained so much more. I will love you forever and always, with all my heart and soul."

"Maeve," the Magistrate said. "Do you take Gaston to be your husband?"

She grinned. "Hell yeah, I do."

"Gaston, do you take Maeve to be your wife?"

"Without a doubt, I do."

The Magistrate nodded once and said, "You are now husband and wife. You may kiss your bride."

He didn't have to tell him twice. Gaston swept Maeve into his arms and kissed her like she was the last drop of blood on the planet. She returned the passion, wrapping her arms around his neck and slipping her tongue into his mouth. They made out like teenagers beneath the high school bleachers until the Magistrate finally cleared his throat.

Gaston released Maeve and slipped his hand into hers. "Apologies. I've waited more than one hundred years for this, and I got carried away."

"Feel free to get carried away any time you want," Maeve said.

They walked arm in arm up the aisle and into

the house for the celebration. Ethan and Addy gave toasts, and of course, Jane had a bit to say. She cleared her throat and held up her glass to Maeve. "I am so happy you two found each other. Maeve, you've gotten this mysterious, tipsy vampire to open up more than any of us ever could have, and I have never seen him smile so much. Welcome to the family. We're all glad you're here."

The living guests dined on filet mignon while the vampires were treated to Gaston's secret stash of rare AB Negative. Jazz music filled the air, and Gaston couldn't have wiped the smile off his face if his undead life depended on it.

As the party began to wind down, the Magistrate approached. "Congratulations to both of you again."

"Thank you for officiating," Maeve said. "It's pretty cool to be married by the Magistrate himself."

He bowed slightly. "It was my pleasure. Anything for the newest member of the Council." He caught Gaston's gaze and arched a brow.

"Is that an official invitation?"

"We have two empty seats. I believe one should go to the vampire who rid New Orleans of a murderous threat such as you did. I would love to welcome you back."

"It would be an honor." Gaston bowed.

"Wonderful. Come in next month to finalize the paperwork. That should give the newlyweds plenty of time to celebrate their union, yes?"

"Plenty of time." Maeve patted Gaston's shoulder. "Thank you."

As the Magistrate walked away, Maeve threw her arms around his neck. "Congratulations! This is wonderful."

"Indeed it is, *ma chérie*. Thanks to you, I've finally gathered my manure into a row."

Maeve laughed. "Yep, you've definitely got your shit together."

"What do you say we boot everyone out and retire to the bedroom before daylight? I want to make love to my bride before the death sleep claims you."

Maeve flashed a seductive grin. "I'd say that sounds fan-flapping-tastic."

ALSO BY CARRIE PULKINEN

Fire Witches of Salem Series

Chaos and Ash

Commanding Chaos

Claiming Chaos

New Orleans Nocturnes Series

License to Bite

Shift Happens

Life's a Witch

Santa Got Run Over by a Vampire

Finders Reapers

Swipe Right to Bite

Batshift Crazy

Collection One: Books 1-3

Collection Two: Books 4 - 7

Crescent City Wolf Pack Series

Werewolves Only

Beneath a Blue Moon

Bound by Blood

A Deal with Death

A Song to Remember

Shifting Fate

Collection One: Books 1-3

Collection Two: Books 4-6

Haunted Ever After Series

Love at First Haunt

Second Chance Spirit

Third Time's a Ghost

Love and Ghosts

Love and Omens

Love and Curses

Collection One: Books 1 - 3

Collection Two: Books 4 - 6

Stand Alone Books

Flipping the Bird

Sign Steal Deliver

Azrael

Lilith

The Rest of Forever

Soul Catchers

Bewitching the Vampire

About the Author

Carrie Pulkinen is a paranormal romance author who has always been fascinated with things that go bump in the night. Of course, when you grow up next door to a cemetery, the dead (and the undead) are hard to ignore. Pair that with her passion for writing and her love of a good happily-ever-after, and becoming a paranormal romance author seems like the only logical career choice.

Before she decided to turn her love of the written word into a career, Carrie spent the first part of her professional life as a high school journalism and yearbook teacher. She loves good chocolate and bad puns, and in her free time, she likes to read, drink wine, and travel with her family.

Connect with Carrie online:
www.CarriePulkinen.com